TRY TO CATCH NUJA

TRY TO CATCH NUJA

by

GERALDINE HUNTER

*Blackie & Co
Publishers Ltd*

A BLACKIE & CO PUBLISHERS PAPERBACK

© Copyright 2002
Geraldine Hunter

First published in 2002

A CIP catalogue record for this title is available from the British Library

Cover design by Chris Winch
Chris@chriswinch.fsnet.co.uk

ISBN 1 903138 35 3

**Blackie & Co Publishers Ltd
107-111 Fleet Street
LONDON EC4A 2AB**

Dedication

In memory of Mary,
who enjoyed this fantasy.

CHAPTER ONE

His brother Arnie had plunked him here on the bleachers with a thermos of coffee, and had gone off to talk horses or cattle or whatever with some acquaintances. This was the third horse meet he'd dragged him to in this cold spring.

"A lot of fresh air and ornery animal flesh will keep your mind off the bottle," he'd said more than several times.

"It's the fresh air and the animal flesh that's put my mind on the bottle," Bridger groaned inwardly.

"These nags are just coming out of their winter lay-around," Arnie had said. "They'll shape up nice for summer. You'll see."

As if he cared to see. Bridger could see him, in a group some distance away. He considered going down to join them, then he reconsidered, thinking he might as well shiver here as listen to more horse talk. Worse, some kid might shove a rope into his hand and ask him to hold his mount.

That had happened at the previous meet and the horse attached to the rope, not wishing to be saddled, had flung his head every which way – nearly dislocating Bridger's arm – and then had swung his rump toward the greenhorn.

Arnie had been able to grab the rope as Bridger retreated, and to give it a strong sharp jerk down, while at the same time the boy had put a well-placed knee against the horse's belly. (These actions appear very persuasive to horse obedience.) To Bridger's excuses, Arnie – always the one to repair a person's ruptured self esteem – had guffawed, "This guy? He's just a little pony!" Then instructively, "You gotta let 'em know who's boss."

Acquiescing unhappily in the proposition that they were "boss", the horse had stood sulkily while the boy enveloped his head in ropes, piled things on top of him, and then mounted to a squeaking of leather and a pinching of cinches that had rather swung Bridger's sympathies to the horse. Not to be completely vanquished, though, and with a venomous glance at Bridger, "little pony" had jerked off in a run two-walk two step – the most speed, it seemed (Bridger had gloated in silence), that they were going to get out of him that day.

Spurning any such repetition, then, Bridger flipped his coat collar up over his ears and settled down to shiver. Trust Arnie to find a local practice one hundred miles from home. He didn't even have his horses with him, and here he was, all caught up with the activity on the track, if activity it could be called. The riders had sorted out some particularisations three-year olds and four-year olds; five-year olds and six-year olds, etc.; under sixty inches and over sixty inches, and then a few ponies – all of no consequence to the horses. Most of them were resisting all attempts to be ridden at all, and more than one seemed determined, if they must go, to take the track sideways. A number had gathered dispiritedly in the centre of the field, and while Bridger commiserated with them, imagining they were as cold and as uncomfortable as he, he heard someone say to his companion, "Hey Viv, look at that horse!"

Bridger broadened his attention. Apparently they had got some horses coerced into the spirit, for six or seven were churning up showers of mud along the track. The farthest one (even scrubbier than the rest) had no rider. Bridger thought the rider must have been thrown, until he noticed the horse was running not on the track, but beyond it, being obscured every so often by clumps of budding bushes. As the winner splashed in to shouts here and there, the scrub, crossing the same parallel on his forest track, drew spontaneous cheers for his neat run. Unimpressed, he meandered off to munch bits of new grass.

Later when all the events had been run, Bridger exhaled his last suffering sigh as the wagons and trailers filed out. Arnie was the last to leave – a chronic routine with him. There wasn't a vehicle in sight by the time they turned onto the paved road. As they drove along the side of the grounds they had just occupied, there grazed the grey horse, all alone.

"Must belong to someone around here," Arnie commented.

In the rainy evenings Bridger spent many hours reading. Either he or Kitty, Arnie's wife, brought books from the library regularly, and Kitty had a little library of her own.

"How come you have so many books on the fur traders?" he asked.

"Well, Marda gave me most of them," she answered. "Her grandfather has a roomful of books and papers – a veritable archive. His father and grand father were both in the fur trade. I find these interesting. Don't you?"

"Yes, I like them," Bridger agreed. "Just reading about the arduous lives these people lived makes you realise what an easy time we have. And the frustrations and delays! I remember Midge and I being so exasperated at a few hours layover waiting for plane connections. We thought we had delays. This – listen to this account of a typical trip to a new area: the canoe – they first have to make their canoe, or take old ones – the canoe gets thrown against the rocks. They get it to shore and repair. Takes two hours. Start again, get two miles.

Have to portage. Two men waiting from another canoe to help carry the pieces of baggage to where they've camped at the other side of portage. A clerk and two men sent to search out a road for next day. Next day the canoes are light loaded with six men each and run down, then back for other baggage. On for three miles, then carry up steep bank. With rain and leakage the canoes get steadily heavier, so that, in time, it takes four men to carry them. In very steep places men haul from above with a line on the bow. Those below rest it on their shoulders. Then up and down for the baggage. Canoes and baggage laid out to dry. For the exhausted men, a dram of rum. They cook flour and sugar for the evening meal. Then the canoes are gummed, and tattered moccasins are repaired. Next day, start all over again. A few good miles, then carry, then run light, then carry, then use line, then gum or repair.

"They lose hours every day, and run out of bark and gum and watape, which they must gather constantly when they aren't fighting the water or the bad ground."

"Their stamina is incredible, isn't it?" he said, looking up, "on three meals of pemmican a day and a pipe every hour or so. Sometimes they get fish at a lake where they camp. Sometimes the Indians trade fish and game for goods, and sometimes help carry at portages – although it's more often the women who help carry. (Kitty snorted.) Yet when these voyageurs arrive from a long trip to a fort, they come in with a dash, paddles flashing, black hair flying, ribbons fluttering."

Bridger paused in admiration, flipping pages. "And then in the Columbia," he went on, "they have also to become trappers. Just look at a brigade! Perhaps fifty

5

men, twenty-five to thirty of them trappers, made up of Canadians (French Canadians), Iroquois from the east and Hawaiians taken from the ships. Maybe twenty-five wives and sixty to seventy children, of which, helpfully, many are old enough to carry guns. Local and regional Indians accompany the party – but don't usually trap. Three hundred to four hundred horses to carry all the people and the equipment (traps, tents, and trade goods. As well, fur packs accumulate as they travel, some of which are cached for the return journey. No food is carried. They live off the land. Wow!

"Then when main camp is established the trappers go out each morning and come back in the evening with the day's returns. Always they are watching for hostile Indians, and are under stricture to trap the furs and keep the peace. When they have trapped out an area, main camp is moved. Their total travels could be nearly four thousand miles!

Kitty had read all these before and, busy with her work, nodded a little absently to his enthusiasm. Bridger realised he was probably hindering her more than anything else and got up to help her prepare supper. As he peeled vegetables, though his mind remained on the private journals that recorded the daily trials and complaints of a long-ago era. These were not only published journals that had been turned in to the respective companies, but also tattered notebooks, scraps of paper, even a piece of animal skin, with entries that gave little or no clue as to the company, area, or year, but eloquently painted the day of the fur hunter and trader:

"Down a low pass, dark walls overhanging. Over rocks, around boulders, then twist into the light through a mesh of slender close-spaced pines. The horses lodge their loads between the trees. Have to unload and repack. Crossed the creek and re-crossed fourteen times. Warm sunshine at this time of day, but freezes hard every night. It gets milder as we get lower, though, and late tomorrow we expect to reach the lake, where the men will meet us with the canoes."

"Very imposing Chief of Snakes invited us to his camp. In each region the Indians keep note of our movements. They know where we are. All were about their everyday living – gathering wood and preparing meals; others smoked in leisure or gambled their possessions; some swam (they are excellent swimmers); others raced horses or rode about – horses all over."

"Came up with the hunters bringing back three deer to camp, when Georges raced past, not even seeing us. Pierre, behind, yelled 'Enemies! Enemies!'. Letting the pack horses go, we raced after. We were the last to arrive and camp was already secured. As we took our place, Chief Trader with his white flag went to meet them. It was a band of Nez Perce under a minor chief who had at first opposed the peace. He was a very fine specimen, and bold. Jean Pierre was left to smoke with them while preparations were made for their all-night stay. All the camp was armed and some of their horses were put with ours as security. They sang and danced most of the night, and in the morning traded a number of skins for rings, awls, axes, knives and blankets. Vermillion and little mirrors were very popular. We got some very fine furs, elk meat, and some horses, one of which looked very much like one of those we had lost a few weeks before."

"Follow the streams, cross and re-cross. Got good lifts, seventy each time – for few days. Many, many buffalo. Ample food, and the hides make boats to cross the river. But we are in Blackfoot country. Keep parties close and horses hobbled, with at least four guards at night. As beaver peter out, send parties in different directions to search out beaver and any scouts for Indian war parties. See figures in distance but they disappear when we pursue. Have come across fires still warm.

"Beaver get scarce, little grass for horses. Work ourselves into impasse and rather than retreat, decide to hack trail through small section. Men, horses, and axes to work. Kieno, one of Kanakas, got his arm slashed. This is hard country for the Sandwich Islanders. The six here were conscripted off the ship at the coast last summer. They must regret leaving their gentle shores. I bathe Kieno's arm in cold water and put loose bandage on. During the night he fell into fever. Put calomine paste on and re-bandage. Old Baptiste is not well, either. Got his woman to make a broth for him. Send hunting party out, rest to work on road. It is much tougher than first hoped.

"Sparse game. The women look after the horses and bring us fresh ones. The men complain. Send Bedden, my second-in-command, with party to hunt mountain sheep. With him, he takes LaLoche. This stratagem separates him and Charbonnais, who fight over their wives. The hunters return in two days with game. The kettles are filled and the camp takes on a little joy. From the high slopes, Bedden also viewed the terrain. Says our road will take us to richer looking quarter. Bedden, from Vermont, is proving responsible and resourceful. This is his first year out here in the far west with the company.

"With luck, the road will be finished tomorrow. Kieno's wound is healing well now. He will be able to do limited work tomorrow. Old Baptiste, too, is better, except for the rheumatism in his legs. Entering my tent, I hear Bedden talking low to one of the guards. I turn in to my blankets and dream of Fort Vancouver, the wide stairs curving up from the common room, the gentlemen's room with comfortable chairs and cheery fire in the grate, and big windows looking out on rolling grass, dotted with trees and grazing horses."

"Almost hypnotising to see the river below gorging through great granite slabs. Five to six men with twenty light horses go first, then the pack-horses, families, then the leader and six to seven men at rear. It was precarious and took much care and patience to ease along. Children cried and a dog howled dismally as it slipped into a small crevice. With great dexterity, Scawa hauled it up again. Down from the height, we gain wide ground only to find ourselves floundering around in muskeg. Much pulling and hauling the horses to firmer ground. Wet with mud and sweat, we rounded the shoulder of the mountain to find we couldn't completely avoid a burned area. Slog through a tongue of blackened muck to reach green again. Finally found a reasonably level and safe place. Set camp with tempers flaring, and women ready to tear each other's hair."

After the first incident of the grey horse, Arnie dragged Bridger to more practices, going forty miles this way, twenty the other, with the two horses he was shaping up for summer. Bridger had to admit they were getting more amenable; they would run with less head-shaking and buttock-swinging as a precondition, and they were beginning to put some real intent into their running.

"See!" Arnie said when Bridger observed this to him. "You're beginning to see the difference in horses and horse behaviour. You're really watching them."

"Ya, ya, ya," Bridger chanted to himself as Arnie went on. "Soon you'll even like them."

"He had to say that, didn't he!" Bridger winced silently.

It was true that, after he had built sufficient resistance to the weather, he had begun to watch them with a degree of interest. He admitted this to Arnie, "Especially that grey one. But they never brush him down. They don't even bring him. How does he get to these things?"

"Oh, it's turned out to belong to Malcolm's bunch," Arnie laughed. "They've got themselves another ancient ways traveller."

"A what?" Bridger asked.

"It's an Indian legend. Belongs to their tribe. They say a grey horse saved the life of an ancestor of theirs a hundred – or ranging up to two hundred years ago – and when he returns they have to repay the debt. Every so often they dredge up a grey horse and pretend it's their legend in the flesh. It's just a gag. They have a lot of fun with it. At least those two do, the Braids. They're Scottish on their father's side. That's Malcolm, and the one with the reddish hair is his brother. He and another brother only come rarely. The darker, silent one is a cousin from upcountry. I haven't seen him since he was a kid. At least I didn't recognise him at that meet upcountry, earlier this year; he must have been there, because the horse was there."

So that's what all the remarks were about! Bridger had thought they were prompted by the appearance of the grey horse. His winter coat was coming out in gobs, some of which hung in puffs from his hide. His mane lay along his neck in knots, and his tail, too, was tangled with burrs and interlaced with bits of thorn vine.

"That still doesn't say how the horse gets to these meets," Bridger said.

"Oh, someone brings him," Arnie assured him.

"We've seen him still there after everyone else has gone," Bridger reminded him.

"They come back later and get him."

"And trust him not to go away in the meantime?"

"Oh, they've got him tethered some way," Arnie said with irritation. "They're slick at that."

Bridger thought that was a lot of trouble to go to for a gag. But then he reminded himself that "horse" people can be funny – evidence Arnie: in this (to Bridger) draggingly cold spring (Arnie said it was a mild spring) there wasn't a practice anywhere that he'd miss. "Why can't he just practise at home?" Bridger had complained to Kitty, who had explained that the competition was necessary to the practising. And Malcolm and his dark cousin, whose name was Chick, seemed hardly less driven, for they were often at the same gathering, doing all the fast-moving, attention-getting actions. Chick, though, also did a slower type of equestrianism on one of his horses, obviously a favourite, a tall red animal that moved as smoothly as a dancer.

"That horse even crosses its feet!" Bridger exclaimed one day.

"That's a part of "dressage", they call it," Arnie answered. "It was trained to do that. But I think that horse will do most of this stuff by itself, as, long as Chick is on its back."

Malcolm, who was sitting close, turned his head and said, "That's just about right. It's the horse that's the artist. He only needs a prompting when he wants to go one way and Chick the other. The two of them understand each other. If only we could tune in to Chick as well! They make a good team."

"They make a good picture, even in work-type outfitting," Bridger thought. "What a picture it would be with Chase in a bright green saddle blanket and green ribbon braided in his mane, and Chick decked out in beautifully cut Spanish velvet, with a green cummerbund."

Despite the touch of class, Bridger was willing to miss any gatherings he could. "I've been all over this Fraser Valley of yours," he complained again to Kitty. "I'll do the washing and make the dinner if you'll take one for me."

"Well, we're all going to the Sunday picnic," she said, "but I'm afraid you're for the rest, Bridge."

"Kind of early for a picnic, isn't it? It's only mid-May."

"Well, we have them. Some years it's good, some years bad. I admit, though, I'd like it to dry out some, myself. Maybe the gods will relax their stern countenances by Sunday and permit a little sunshine."

The spirits of Stolo Prole decided to smile broadly. Under a glowing sun, T'laguna commanded the mountains that ranged the northern horizons of Matsqui: white-headed Baker sat his throne serenely in the Cascades southeast.

Several men on horses dragged rakes or pieces of metal around the track to level somewhat the rough spots. The atmosphere was jovial: filled with cheerful interchanges. The affair was an informal picnic meet of two or three clubs, with ribbons for everybody and for every old plug (as Arnie put it) that wandered onto the track. "Look!" a hoot and a laugh from someone holding up a white third ribbon, "Alphonse came in."

"Did you get behind and push him across?" someone hooted back.

Not all were so happy, though. Maggie, Arnie's eight-year old, complained about her colourless ribbon.

"You didn't do the barrels right," brother Gus explained. "You have to go right, left, left or left, right, right."

"I went right," Maggie insisted.

"I know you went right, but right was wrong then," Gus explained. "Besides, you got a white ribbon."

"You got a red ribbon," she pouted.

"That's because I did it right," Gus shouted.

Maggie slapped at him, and Kitty intervened.

Malcolm's group was lively with the centuries-old horse bit that had been resurrected again this year, and the grey ran around the outside of the track and beat all the other horses. This was actually the first time Bridger had seen him make a complete circuit, so now the horse had proved himself not only to Bridger but to all present. (Of course, he had no rider, so perhaps the lack of weight cancelled the distance.)

Whatever, the feat brought a fresh renewal of jocularity, one that lasted into the meal. All the while, the smell of roasting salmon and beef had been wafting through the air, and later the smell of coffee was added. Plates of salmon, beef, salad, fistfuls of buns, cups of coffee were being carried to all parts of the grounds. Somehow, with Gus, Bridger found himself seated close to Malcolm. The grey's run was still a lively subject, but soon other topics slipped in and the pivotal point of conversation moved away, leaving them on the fringe.

Bridger had asked Kitty one day about the story of the grey horse.

"Oh, it's very vague and different according to who tells it," she had answered. "You should ask Malcolm. He tells a good story."

So here was Malcolm, in a group somewhat removed from the big crowd. Bridger seized the opportunity and asked if he would tell him the grey horse legend.

"Sure," Malcolm said jovially. "Well this ancestor of ours, Whantoos, who fancied himself a sort of seer – and had his followers – got lost while hunting. He fell down a slope and got lodged in a tangle of forest that seemed to grow arms around his lower body. A rock on one side of him was absolutely smooth: on the other side, a rock all

14

pitted and mossy and a branch waving above, together excited a hope of escape. It proved to be a false hope as he alternately strained for the unreachable branch and clawed at the pitted rock, to get only handfuls of moss. His hands became bloody and throbbing, his body weak with exhaustion and confinement. He knew he would die, and wondered whether it would be when the sun wore high, and beat mercilessly on him or when the night came cold, and chilled him to the bone. All the time, even semi-conscious, he could hear the tantalising sound of a brook, and he longed for a drink of water.

"At all times he was confronted with the hillside opposite. It stood so beautifully green, silent: so impassively unhelping, until in a sudden moment Whantoos saw a horse standing there, utterly still, as though it had grown up out of the ground. It was looking straight at him. He urged it to come to him. How had he ever seen it? Its cover was only slightly less than that surrounding it. He spoke, as he thought, barely above a whisper, afraid the sound of his voice would scare it away.

"Slowly the horse moved, picking its way carefully, and bent its head to him. No hallucination, then! Whantoos grasped the mane, but it pulled painfully from his hands as the horse raised its head.

"The horse backed away and turned as though it would go. 'No, no!' Whantoos pleaded – unnecessarily, for the horse backed in as if it knew exactly what to do. Reaching high, Whantoos grabbed its tail in his only chance. He must hold on through the pain. The first loosening made his head swim crazily, and then he saw blackness.

"He came to with his face crushed against the undergrowth. It took him some time to know where he was, and when he could raise himself a little on his arm, he saw the horse a short distance away, eating grass, completely unruffled, and swishing now and again its blood-matted tail.

"While Whantoos recovered, eating berries and roots, the horse, a gelding, never roamed and eventually carried the hunter home. The villagers rejoiced and, stimulated by such an amazing rescue, regarded the grey as a little more than natural. Further, though he served Whantoos as his master, he sometimes would halt unmovingly to gaze over tumbled canyons, or to contemplate distant blue hills – looking, always looking."

"Looking for what?" Bridger asked in the silence of the abrupt ending.

Malcolm shrugged his shoulders. "For a sign he could return?" he suggested.

"Up there?" Bridger asked, pointing skyward.

"Actually," Malcolm turned the levity aside, "they found out later he came from the south – the lands around the Columbia River. He was a *real* horse, and his need is the legendary physical obligation of our immediate family, since we are in Whantoos' direct line of descent.

"But as to all these supernatural attributions," he started again with the relish of the true story-teller, "the most widely accepted and embraced is the one that had the grey horse taking Whantoos to a great tent, and walking forward into the entrance. As Whantoos tried to get off, but couldn't, the opening gave way to tall white birch trees standing on either side of a grassy way laid with rich robes. These were blankets of dog and goat hair, dyed crimson, made and traded by the coast tribes. The platform ahead was laid with the same robes, and it held a beautifully carved chest which was draped with the finest pelts of beaver, marten, fox. Behind, from a lattice-work of willow branches hung a panel of tawny grizzly bear. Against these golden pelts stood elegantly polished spears and bows, and a staff carved with symbols of some power. Also on the dias, standing at one end of the chest was a large white wolf. Its four big paws held the floor confidently; it held its head raised, alert and in calm control."

Malcolm paused to take a drink of coffee, then went on. "The elders of that time held in memory an earlier, and sadly lamented chief called White Wolf, and at this "revelation" many decriers of Whantoos became willing to allow that he did have some visionary power, and they adopted it to mean that their beloved White Wolf would return at some future time as an even greater chief; the followers of Whantoos, on the other hand, believed this future chief would be in his line of descendants."

"Was Whantoos a chief?" Bridger asked.

"Only a very minor one."

"Ummh. So as in most things there were, and are, two streams of thought."

"Oh, there's a third," Malcolm tittered. "Some think he had imbibed too many fermenting berries or maybe had got a snatch of the whites' fire-water."

"And what do you believe?" Bridger asked. "Was Whantoos a portender or a pretender?"

Malcolm merely threw out his hands and laughed, "I like the berry bit."

"What we *know*," broke in a voice that Bridger recognised as Chick's, "is that one of us must pay Whantoos' debt to the grey, since he was never offered the opportunity to return the good deed himself."

Chick sat in the comparative darkness of the shade and he spoke with a matching sombreness.

"In a 'time' sense then," Bridger said, "this is almost a contemporary legend."

"Oh, yes," Malcolm agreed. "After all, the horse is a newcomer in our occupation!"

"Only a little less new than the white man," Chick said, his sombre tone deepening along with the shadow on his face.

CHAPTER TWO

With the weather turning good, Arnie started on the new fencing. Some immediate repairs were needed, as the cattle had got out of the far corner into the second field, which was growing for hay. Arnie was furious, but Bridger found himself almost happy to chase cows back and to pound posts, even in a light rain.

Arnie was not to be cheated of all his several practices, though, and of two events scheduled for the same day, he chose the closer. After a poor turnout because of bad weather locally, he decided he could make the second part of the other one. Despite Bridger's protests they were presently headed east along the freeway. When they arrived at the grounds, it was obvious that that practice also had been called off. Three outfits were there: a truck and a horse trailer and two single trucks. One of these, considerably removed – from the others, Bridger recognised as Chick's. He had come to know that Chick was not always brooding and intense: he could be pleasantly talkative. Arnie fell into conversation with the men closeby, and after a moment of greeting Bridger meandered over to Chick's truck.

As always, Chick was working with his horse. This time, though, he was grooming, and the horse was the grey. To Bridger's further surprise, the grey was accepting the grooming with the utmost patience, even with willingness. Every knot was combed out of the mane; the grey coat lay satiny smooth over his body; the skimpy tail flared modestly.

Chick looked up at his approach.

"What is this?" Bridger asked.

Chick threw his hands wide. "I got so tired of practising – Chase did, too ("Well sometimes it *does* happen," Bridger thought.) that I just had to do something else."

The grey moved away and Chick rolled a cigarette (though he had tailor-mades in his pocket), lit it, and took a seat on a nearby stump.

"Have you been here all day?" Bridger asked.

"Almost," he answered. "I came this morning. Got some good practising in – Chase likes this kind of ground. It's a little damp. I loaded him up and went away for lunch, but came back. Others have come and gone – had a little competition with two or three of them. Hasn't rained much here, although apparently it has other places close around."

His voice bespoke his disappointment.

Bridger nodded in sympathy. "Too late to start now, though," he suggested.

"Oh Yeah," Chick answered. "Guess I'll go home."

As though he had heard and had to have his run for the un-materialised event, the grey left the trees and took off across the field adjoining the track. The sun, making one of its peek-a-boos, picked up the new lustre of his hide and gleamed against the coal-bits in the pale ash colour of his coat.

"Who says he isn't pretty?" Bridger remarked.

As the horse swerved back, the sun sent a bronze ripple across the yellow tips of his mane and rather exploded into fine copper streaks through the brownish brush of his tail.

Bridger glanced towards Chick, who also had caught the colour display.

"Blood on his tail," Chick said.

Small horses had run around the track; big horses had run around the track; horses had run around barrels and poles and two or three had run away to unmolested corners, pursued by pedestrian cowboys. Light carts, the genteel of the show, had swished through, drawn by nicely-groomed horses exhibiting elegant footwork. The cumbersome chuck-wagons had rocked and clattered their half–mile. With all this, the dust had risen in clouds and now hung suspended like a solid part of the air.

Bridger had spent part of the time in the stands, part assisting Arnie when neither Gus nor Kitty was around, and part on the grass or the gravel, moving among the participants: drivers and wagons, riders and horses. It was debatable which were the more interesting, the human competitors running their races again in enlivened dialogue or the equine competitors, completely disinterested in anything except searching for accessible patches of grass; those tied so they couldn't get grass watched longingly those who could. One horse had got the tail of his win ribbon in his teeth and was about to chew, it up when his young rider rescued it. The purple rosette was still intact and shiny but the ribbon ends were ragged, sodden, and green-mottled.

"Mom," she wailed, "look what Banky did!"

As the chariots began wheeling toward the gate Bridger made his way back to the truck. He entertained a silly hope that, Arnie's categories all completed, they might leave now before the final efflux. Arnie, of course, had no such intention. Bridger sat on the ground against the wheel of the truck.

"Boy, look at Joe swing into the lead," Arnie exclaimed. "And Cam is trying to leave the others... What the hell is that?"

Other electric remarks filled the air: "What's that?" "Is that a bird?"

Bridger leaped to his feet to search for the object of these exclamations. The chariots were trundling around the track. Nothing was impeding them. No bird of any size.

Then he saw what they saw. Outside the track on the far side of the grounds flashes of colour and flying feathers could be glimpsed as something sped past bushes and trees. A bird that big! As the apparition gained open ground, it proved to be a four-legged beast of magnificent colours – reds, yellows, blues, whites. A grand tuft of feathers, nearly two feet high, bobbed on its head. The black mane flew and two feathered streamers flew from the bright blue clubbed tail.

"It's a horse," someone said. "I bet that's Jiff Peter's work."

"Yeah," others joined in. "He's done it again."

The near groups started to regale each other with Jiff Peter's exploits. "Remember the time he painted the horse green and put a green Martian on it, with a glass bowl over his head?"

So it went. It was not a good day for the charioteers. The event had started out with an argument between the first group to run and the time-keeper, who had got quite distracted by the gorgeous horse act, and succeeding groups were racing their hearts out to an audience that was only half watching.

Bridger felt much less guilty about his earlier wishes of defection and, unrepentant, pursued his way to the outer flanks of the crowd. As he headed toward a quiet spot he had earmarked, he came upon Chick, alone with three horses. The side of the truck was adorned with the ribbons his group had collectively won. He smiled at Bridger's sign of approval. He had done well with both his horses, the red proving a beast of wide talents.

"Where are the others?" Bridger asked.

"Oh, they're over at the fence watching Malcolm in the chariots."

"Mmh," Bridger responded. "Bad day for the chariots."

They both laughed, and Bridger said, "I can't take any more. I'm heading for that quiet spot of grass over there."

"Looks like you'll have to share it with the grey," Chick said.

"Yeah," Bridger flung back.

At that moment the strangest thought went through his head. He almost turned back to voice it to Chick, but kept on walking.

Later when they had arrived home in their different vehicles, and Arnie and Bridger had got the animals pastured, they came in to find Kitty taking a load of washing from the machine. She put another one in, all the while talking excitedly about the coloured horse. "Jiff really did a magnificent job, didn't he?" she ended.

"Where were you?" Bridger asked.

"I was at the fence. I got a really good look."

"That was one fancy horse,'" Arnie allowed.

"A Nez Perce war horse!" Kitty emphasised.

"Was it?" Bridger asked.

"Yes. Straight out of the historical description in the book. Don't you remember?"

"Can't say I do, but nobody would have any hesitancy making it an Indian horse."

"If I didn't have so much to do, I'd go over now and see it close, before he gets the paint off," Kitty said.

Those who did try to see it close-up, however, were disappointed. Jiff said he didn't do it, and showed all his unadorned horses as proof.

At any rate, the affair provided a lively subject of conversation during the following week and into Kitty's barbecue one evening. As good smells and smoke smells mingled in the air, puzzles and explanations gave way to tales.

"Jiff always says he didn't do it," was the general remark.

"At first," Kitty amended. "Afterwards he parades his handiwork around for all to see."

"That's true," several agreed.

"And why not?" someone added.

"That's what I find so odd about its quick disappearance," Bridger put in at that. "Why would anyone do all that work on a horse, only to have it seen for just a few seconds?"

"Jiff wouldn't," several said at once, remarking back and forth on incidents that attested to Jiff's eagerness to proclaim his achievements.

"Then who is the artist in our midst?" someone finally asked.

"Yeah who?" was the multiple response. The company debated this, then trailed to other subjects as the hamburgers and coffee were passed around. Twilight turned to dark and the young kids climbed into sleeping bags on the porch. The older ones formed a little group of their own and propounded their own versions of the coloured horse, the rodeo, and all other things.

The campfire flared and sent sparks flying high. Inevitably the horse got back into the conversation again, but the tone had changed.

"Another thing, whoever did it had an awful lot of luck getting the horse seen only for its run – I mean nobody saw it arriving at its starting point, which was halfway across a big field, or from its ending point, from where we assume it ran down that little hill to the road and into a waiting truck. And well-trained to do it by itself, too!"

"Well, there's a lot of cover both ways," one voice reasoned. "It could be done."

"You'd still need a lot of luck," the first insisted. Others agreed with this view but, seemingly, everyone ran out of words at this point, leaving only the fire sparking into the darkness.

"So – 'ees maybee the grey horse!" The words, from Rosalita, Leo's Mexican wife, fell expectantly into the silence. Now that the fanciful thought had been voiced, there was no reticence to pursue it.

"But the grey was there all the time, wasn't he?" someone asked.

"Who knows?" spoke another. "Who was looking for the grey when that was going on?"

"Anyway," Kitty said, "the Indian legend does place him from the Columbia River area."

"Which means he is aptly adorned," came another voice. "But it's his other attributes that excite the imagination."

"Oh come on," Arnie broke in. "You guys don't believe in that Indian tale! Even Malcolm doesn't believe that."

"Oh yes he does," averred another. "Even his father does."

"No," a third said, "his father says it's the grey that spirited Garth Kilcratchie back across the border a quarter mile ahead of the English."

While a general chuckle went round at this, Arnie, the sole realist in this seductive setting, intoned deprecatingly, "Great spirits! Lowland border sprites!"

"And sentimental visits," put in a soft voice.

The others around the fire turned their eyes to the speaker, a man older than the rest of them, and completely unselfconscious in his assertion.

"My grandfather had a favourite horse when he was younger, a big grey Percheron. The others – I was the youngest of my family – would exchange knowing glances when grandfather would tell me of Major's visits, but one summer night when I lay awake with the warm air pouring through the open window, I heard a clop, clop, clop on the tractor road beside the house and the petering off along the fence. As had always been done, sometimes we would close the front gates and let the horses graze around the house and road, and between the trees. This was Major's favourite area, my father said. He would nibble at the grass and wait for Grandfather to come out with apples.

"That night, I went to the window and peered into the darkness. A shadowy form merged with the shadows of trees that edged the road. A shadowy tail swished. I never told my family that. They wouldn't have believed me."

"Probably it was one of the other horses," someone suggested.

"No. We didn't have any big draft horses at this time. The farm had been cut down; only the fence on the other side of the tractor road remained as the western boundary of our property against the edge of town. The horses we had were fenced in, in the remaining fields at the back."

"Still you admit it was shadowy," the person persisted.

"Shadowy, but in the light from the kitchen window I could make him out. It was old Major," the narrator said, unshakable.

"Anyway, this is a little different," a fresh voice spoke. "This horse, so we understand, comes armed with a record of debits and credits."

"If he has debits for Malcolm's bunch, why did he show his "notice" to the whole countryside?" Another asked logically. "Why not just to the family concerned?"

The first speaker had no answer but a third voice suggested, "Maybe there are debtors in this transaction that aren't even aware."

"Mm umh!" Leo flung his hand in agreement. "Spanish legend has a horse like this. It pops up through the centuries, giving loyalty, other times demanding it –

but this only in connection with a mare, a certain mare that he searches out without error. And the people who get drawn into his life he knows more about than they know themselves. Those who owe him will help in his search, or its resolution, despite themselves."

"What things does he know, and how does he let them know he knows?" Someone giggled.

"He shows them!" Leo answered. "Like the uncountable riches beyond an unmapped ocean that one conquistador saw.

"There are many versions – and many settings – like the bedouin who saw the castles and mosques that would rise under the Moors in Spain."

"The Moors! Out of Africa, then, an Arabian horse," came an exclamation. "I read about the dark charger that took the prized mare of this Ibn el Baakar, or some such. I can recall the scene set in the book at any instant, and I even think I can feel the cool desert air as she races off in the night, her flaxen mane flying like white mists in the scant light of a hazy moon."

"Si," Rosalita answered spontaneously. "Thees story from Mexico ees like that. Long time ago when Santa Fe was not old."

"Santa Fe?" Bridger interrupted.

"Si. Thees ranchero had beautiful amarillo – uh," she looked at her husband, "yea-lo?"

"Yellow," he agreed.

"Yea-lo mare weeth long white hair." She drew her hand down her neck.

"Mane," Leo prompted.

"Si, mane. El ranchero have her – for carreege (which he bring all way from Mexico City at many pesos) and ees beautiful peecture when they go to mission for supplies – prancing yea-lo mare and shiny black carreege.

"Thees horse they see in distance, black with white on side. He thair many times and he watch. El señor first try to catch him with lasso to tame, but he cannot. Then try to shoot him in fear he take his favourite mare – but horse always evade him so fas, seem like he disappear. Indian slaves look after him – wis-wistful.

"One day carreege is readied and la señora, alone, take reins. She no supposed to. Horse ees tempenta –"

"Temperamental," Leo supplied.

"Si. Horse she frighten and run off with carreege. Thees black horse run fas over plain, come up and run beside her till she slow down and stop. – El mayordomo from hacienda seeing her and racing fas after. When he get close, black horse go. He tie his horse to carreege and take reins.

"La señora tell him she sorry she cause incident, and she know she owe black horse, too.

"At his look she explain she say 'too' because she has feel before that he no want black horse caught or hurt, and she ask what ees he owe thees strange horse.

"He move his head back and forth and say all he know ees he keep seeing ship leaving busy port which he somehow know ees Seville. On wharf, grand señor is yelling 'Princessa! Princessa!' as beautiful horse races back and forth, and whinnies frantic in answer to same cries from ship raising slow sail.

"El mayordomo no understan. He only know to take obstacles out of way of thees horse.

"Nex day, black horse come close to rancho. Yea-lo mare in corral leap over fence and they go weeth dust rising after them.

"Both la señora and el mayordomo feel glad horses escape, but quick to worry about wrath of Don Ameliano, who soon returning from mission, loaded with supplies and fine things that have come on the conducta. And arrive weeth the conducta, Don Ameliano's brothair, over year on trail from Mexico. Doña Ameliano thinks of the silver tableware, and the red silk dress and satin slippers Don Ameliano would so happy arrive home weeth, and she dread to tell him thees news.

"When she did, el mayordomo say that now Don Ameliano back, he would start in morning and search for mare.

"'I weel go weeth you,' el señor say.

"'But he is best tracker in country,' la señora say fervently, 'and rancho need one of you.'

"'My brothair weel stay,' he say. 'I weel bring back my mare, and I weel keel that mustang.'

"La senora cast fearful glance at el mayordomo. He go out with no expression on face.

"In few days they come back weethout horse. 'What happen?' la señora ask, feared he keel both horses.

"'We found them,' su esposo answer, 'but they get away. Nevair have I been so clumsy! Every time I go to shoot, something happen: my musket misfire, my foot slips, my horse shie. Only time shot touched him, so far away maybe not even bullet, but stone that bounce against leg. Last I see, they heading into mountains. No use to follow farther.'

"Anger and frus-frustrate, he stalk into house. Doña Ameliano follow, after she exchange look of knowing with el mayordomo, who pick up reins and walking horses to barn. He no understan why he did thees theeng, but he knew he would do it again if he mus.

"And someone weel do it for thees grey horse," Rosalita added seriously.

A burst of chuckles came from the smiling faces around the campfire. Bridger joined in. In this atmosphere it was an enchanting thought.

Bridger saw Chick a couple of days later. Arnie had dragged him to an auction where, wearying of the endless halters and other tack, he retreated outdoors. Outside, Chick was leaning against a truck and holding a bottle of pop. "Too hot for me in there," he said.

Bridger grimaced in agreement. "Arnie's sticking in there. He has his eye on something."

"Yeah, I was looking for some tack – for a friend," Chick replied.

"I thought for a moment there you were going to say for the grey horse."

Chick laughed, and following in the joking mood, Bridger said, "The other night around the campfire we decided for a while that the grey was also the Nez Perce war horse."

Chick smiled, nodding his head up and down.

"You decided the same thing?" Bridger asked.

"At first," he answered, "but it wasn't him – at least not the way he is now."

"How could you know that?" Bridger laughed, "in all those paints and feathers?"

"I know the way he moves, the way he holds his head," he said with absolute surety.

"You're being serious now."

"Of course. I'm always serious about the grey horse."

After a moment of consternation Bridger said, "Let's talk about the real horse, then – the one that got to Whantoos in the nick of time. How did your people find out that he was from the Columbia River?"

"You might say all our horses came from the Columbia region," Chick answered. "From the Shawhaptans, Palouse, Cayuse – all Nez Perce. They sifted up through the Flatheads, Okanagans, Kootenay to the east.

"But this particular horse was recognised by a man from a Columbia tribe. He had hired on with a white exploring party – fur traders seeking an alterative trail northward. When they came through our village my people, though not surprised to see whites, were surprised to see a member of a band from so far south. Not many individuals accompanied past neighbouring territory, you know. He, for his part, was very surprised to see the grey gelding, one of the best horses of Iquaq, he said, who sold it to Scasa,who lost it on a beaver hunting trip two years before."

"Beaver hunting," Bridger pondered. "The Indians didn't take horses to beaver?"

Chick shook his head negatively.

"You mean a trapping party?"

Chick nodded affirmatively this time.

"Columbia trapping parties," Bridger mused over the information while Chick raised the bottle to his mouth.

"Too bad it didn't have a name, this horse on the Columbia."

"It did," Chick responded. "They called it 'Tnustchaen'."

"How come you never told anyone this before?" Bridger asked, surprise in his voice.

"They know." Chick's voice held a little chuckle at Bridger's ignorance. "Malcolm says there is a reference to it in your journals of the fur trade."

"What!" The statement took Bridger aback, and Chick finished his pop, put the bottle in the back of the truck, and made a move to the door of the vehicle before, apparently, Bridger had assimilated the news and accepted that the chat was concluded.

"Aren't you going to load your horse first?" Bridger, recovered, was allowed his turn at surprises.

Chick looked at him in puzzlement, and Bridger pointed to the grey standing off on bare ground beyond a parking railing. He had just caught sight of the horse himself.

"Well, you just never know where he's going to show up, do you?" Chick said. "I know he'll leave the same way he came." He got into the truck, and with a wave pulled away. Several other vehicles left at the same time, setting up a cloud of dust.

It was too hot to go back inside, even though Arnie wouldn't be out for ages. Bridger thought the horse would have disappeared sometime during the last few minutes, but when he looked again, there he stood with the dust settling on him, not a blade of grass to eat, and only Bridger to look at – or *not* to – look at: he was studiously ignoring him, yet somehow impelling, not just his strict attention, but his whole consciousness. Bridger could see greenery, mounted forms winding through the greenery: a trail that ascended steeply, rocks bouncing away, horses slipping.

The next few days they worked on the fencing and repaired one of the barn doors. Then Arnie left Bridger with some further repairs while he went off to some cattle meeting. Bridger did the small job, but found there wasn't nearly enough lumber for the big repair work. He went into the house to ask Kitty what she wanted done, but the house was empty . He sat on the chesterfield and soaked in the unusual silence. A short wall led off the far side of the room to a sun-room: on the wall was a picture of a grey horse, a favourite of Arnie's. It had been dead for many years, but it still held a place in his affections.

From outside came the sound of Kitty yelling at Doddie to get his shoes.

Bridger had told her about his meeting with Chick.

"How come you never told me that Whantoos' horse was once a brigade horse, known by name, and referred to in the journals?" He had asked her.

"*They* say he was a brigade horse, and it's believable, but they've never offered or identified any paper or journal that contained this reference. They don't care, you know, whether we believe them or not," she had answered. "Marda says she thinks she has read such a reference at one time but she doesn't know where. She's looked and looked for it but can't find the mention she seems to remember. She figures she probably got other references mixed up in her mind: there are lots of them, as you know.

"As for the name, Marda did write Malcolm's spelling of it down, but I can never remember it. What is it?"

Bridger had had to retreat, a little sheepishly. "I can't remember myself. It was like 'ch ch tsk tsk' or something."

Kitty had laughed. "Well you can be on the lookout for this ch ch cha yourself. You might be the one to find it."

Now the door banged as Kitty came into the house and proceeded across the kitchen to the dining-room door as Bridger yelled to her and told her about the lumber.

"Well, there's nothing you can do about it," she said. "Here's your chance to do some exploratory reading. Arnie won't be back till late this evening. I've got to go Bridger, I'm taking Doddie to get summer shoes, and I have to get things for the other kids, too."

She picked up her purse and car keys as Doddie opened the back door. "No, no, Doddie, we're going! Go back out! Make yourself lunch, Bridge," she flung back. Doddie squealed goodbye and the door slammed behind them.

Fortified with a pot of coffee and a couple of sandwiches, Bridger started off to read with a certain satisfaction. Maybe he really would come across the very mention. Soon, though, he was faced with the reality of the numbers against it.

Horses! Horses by the thousands! Horses of beauty, of sagacity, loyalty, stamina, courage. How was he to find a clue to this range scrub of unusual persistence, this Indian grey, this Spanish mustang? For, though nearly two hundred years removed, the grey of Whantoos had to be a Spanish horse. No other stock mixed with the

Andalusian strain in all the western half of the continent. Earlier, in the seventeenth century, from Santa Fe, Spain's most northern settlement in interior North America, started the great unintended migration of this unusual beast northward to tribe after tribe.

Fleet! Regal! Snorty! Yet quickly gentled to carry loads that were previously divided between the dogs and the squaws; to carry the Indians themselves to the buffalo hunt, to the battle; to endow them with a splendour heretofore unknown. Oh welcome intruder!

Further, the horse became to the Indian a valuable trading commodity among his own peoples and with the whites in the north. Those whites were grateful for the help of the Indian horse in the western reaches of the fur routes; in the Columbia River tracts, they recognised it as the backbone of the enterprise. In this land where the Indian was not wont to trap assiduously for the whites, the whites needed the Indian horse to trap for themselves, and had it not been for the Indian horse (courtesy of the Spanish horse), the trappers could not have covered such extensive distances as they did to reap those rich harvests of furs. Thus the horse, which enabled the Spanish to make their vast conquests in the New World, slipped out of their express control (becoming the one blessing the Indian received from the white invaders) and, ironically, made profits for the enemy in the misty lands of the north.

Out of all those magnificent beasts, then, whether they groaned under packs or carried riders in opulent parade, *he* had set himself to find the one horse that wouldn't be vanquished by any nation.

CHAPTER THREE

They did more on the barn, and more on the fencing, and progressed while the repair urge was on to some carpentry for Kitty, in the house. In his spare time – and with the return of the rain there was more of it – Bridger continued his reading and – research, but with a diminishing enthusiasm.

"You know," he said to Kitty when she came in one afternoon with two more books, one tied with string to keep the pages together, "I'm really getting tired of reading this stuff."

"Yeah, I know how it gets," she responded, "but we'll be glad to have something to read tonight. I think the skies are really going to open up."

She put the books on the table. "These are from Marda. I was at her place today, and she's hot on her own research project. She says ever since the barbecue something's been twanging around in her head. She'd never heard that story of Rosalita's before and it twigged a memory of an account she read somewhere, years ago, about two horses, not one. She's been going through the mess of books and papers her grandfather's got in his attic. It's really an archive, but it's not catalogued in any way. She thinks she has the likely pile isolated, though."

In the evening, Bridger delved into one of the books. Kitty took the other one. Later in the quiet, Bridger looked up from the page. The rain Kitty had spoken of was slapping against the windows. Kitty sat in an easy chair, engrossed in her book. The kids' voices floated up from the roc-room. Arnie had started a fire, which was spitting cheerfully in the grate, and he sat on the chesterfield, facing the fire, his back to Bridger seated at the dining room table. Arnie wasn't watching the fire, though, Bridger noticed. His head was turned toward the picture of his horse, at which he gazed steadily, lost in some memory. Did Arnie ever hear the clop clop of those big hooves frisking into the field that was once open to the barn?

Grey limbs stretching out, hind legs closing powerfully, thrusting forward the sleek body – a smaller grey this (maybe not even grey), faster than the wind across arid flats.

The scene slipped away from Bridger. Arnie's reverie had slipped away, too. He was now working leisurely on a leather halter, measuring out holes for the buckle.

Bridger wished he could feel as leisurely. He hadn't imagined that scene: it had laid itself before him, unbidden, stirring up a fresh sense of enchantment, but intensifying his frustration. He had read himself nearly cross-eyed with no results, and Marda's efforts were likely to be as unproductive as his and Kitty's. "If only your clues weren't so vague," he silently confronted that grey phantom. "Besides, what's it got to do with me? I'm not in this."

After the rain, the next day came warm, and the following one, hot. Actually it was a break from the reading stalemate when Arnie insisted Bridger go with him to take a young horse up the valley.

Of course it took all day. Arnie delivered the horse and talked for two hours, then meandered along roads till he came to a field that held an unfenced track. Three or four persons were working out their horses in various exercises. Arnie recognised one of the vehicles and pulled in. Though he kept saying he wouldn't stay,

Bridger knew he was set for another two hours: eventually he forgot Bridger was there, and settled himself on a tailgate under the hot sun. A grove of tall trees stood some distance along and Bridger, lacking Arnie's tolerance for the sun's rays, headed for their shade, that was now casting from the west.

The air here was filled with the fragrance of flowers, and he could hear farm animals not far off. Twisting his head, he could just make out the roof of a house on the other side of this light glade. What a pleasant spot! Sitting on the grass, with his back against a tree, he could almost fall asleep. The sound of someone coming caused him to open his eyes. It was Chick leading a horse, not his Chase though. The long tether attached to the halter was folded in his hand the other hand held the rope close. The horse had no saddle. Chick was as surprised to see Bridger there as Bridger was him.

"I didn't see your truck there," Bridger said.

"No, Malcolm took his horse and mine home a little while ago. I was just taking this one home across the fields. Malcolm's son rode him over here bareback, but he went with his dad in the truck. Actually, this old fellow will go home by himself."

Chick had attached the end of the tether to a tree trunk. The horse ranged off a little and Chick took a seat on a fallen log.

As the shadows grew longer they talked about things pleasantly inconsequential. Yet it was an odd perversity that made Bridger stay, for he felt that all along Chick had been waiting for someone, that he had come to meet some particular person. Now as he prodded himself, thinking "Go for heaven's sake," Chick's demeanour swiftly changed, the barely revealed anxiety dropped away; he stood up purposefully and took a step in the direction of his horse, while he slowly took a fold in the rope.

Following his movements, Bridger saw the grey grazing behind. *He* hadn't been there before! Now Bridger was as eager to leave as before he had been reluctant, and he got up, speaking decisive words of goodbye. Chick gave him a look rather like a sympathetic sphinx.

"You seemed to be waiting for someone," Bridger confessed limply and belatedly.

"I thought you were waiting for someone," Chick said. After a few strained seconds, he said, "I guess we were both waiting for someone."

Something like a shiver tickled across Bridger's shoulders as he looked towards him, into woods that stretched darkly ahead. How could this be? Before, he could see right through this little glade.

"Where are we going?" Bridger asked, for his feet, though reluctant, were moving.

"I think," Chick said, "we're attending a little Blackfoot war."

The shiver rafted dawn Bridger's whole body. Chick had reached his horse, and his hand closed on the rope, as though he would leap upon the horse, even though it was still tethered. At the same time, the grey seemed suddenly much closer, in fact seemed to be awaiting him. The prospect was unthinkable! His ineptness joined his fear in a loud protest.

"I'm not going to get on that horse!"

For the first time, amusement flooded Chick's sober countenance, but he said as if soothingly, "You won't be riding the grey."

Bridger looked at his face, solemn again, and realised that he was being drawn along with him, not by him, into this unworldly situation.

The horses' hooves make low thumps on the dirt paths. There are many riders, most up ahead, some to right and some to left, making their way through this light forest. God! This is incredible! He is on a horse! The movements of its body send his hips moving first one way, then the other. His feet dig into its girth, trying to bore a grip. His hands are clasping some very hard-twisted reins. And what is this material covering his legs? He looks down his body to find he is dressed in animal skins. He has a loose top and loose pants, both pieced together in some hazardous way.

He looks for Chick. To his left he sees him. That isn't Chick! But it is! He digs his feet lightly against his horse, hoping he'll move forward. The horse throws his head up and does that dance which keeps him grabbing his mane to hold on. Somehow, though, he has moved up beside Chick's horse. Chick, who isn't Chick, says in a low voice, "Loosen up on the reins. You're pulling on his mouth all the time."

"Oh." He loosens the reins and finds the horse doesn't dance.

"Don't get ahead of me, Chick," he pleads through his pains and lamentations, trying to keep his voice low. Two others turn in their blanket saddles and give them long glances, turning back with gutteral comments.

What? Are they taking them prisoners somewhere? No. Chick isn't acting like a prisoner.

"What are they saying?" Bridger asks him.

"They say they knew they should have left you at home," he whispers. "You never could ride a horse."

"Oh."

On they go. All have long hair, some braided with a feather or two attached here and there. Chick's two feathers bob out of sight each time he turns Bridger's way. Bridger notices his tunic hangs smoothly the joinings are neat and embellished with a trim.

Agonisingly his buttocks pound against the horse, and his legs threaten to petrify in their clinging position, as they go on and on. And on and on...

But the time comes when they see them drawing up ahead. Now how does he stop this horse? If he pulls too tightly, the horse will bounce him all over; if he doesn't pull enough, the horse will walk right on until he meets an immovable object – probably the front end of this group. He gives what he thinks is a gentle pull; the horse goes into jerks and motions that send him, as usual, grabbing for his mane. Chick reaches over, takes the reins lightly, and the horse stops. Thank heavens! Now he prepares to recoup a little of his dignity by swinging off gracefully. He ends up staggering against the legs of the horse, with one hand clutching the mane, while over the top of that furry body he catches the arched eyebrows and knowing exchanged glances of the others.

The group goes into some routine of camping and mercifully leaves him to his own pursuits, which are to relax his muscle-bound legs and revitalise his battered body. It is some time, then, before his mind lets go of his own miseries and he sees that some kind of challenge is being conducted toward Chick. Many, of the men are exhibiting dead fowl, and attention is focused on Chick; it is obviously a good-natured challenge to Chick either to match their prowess or to provide a share of the meal. He cannot see Chick's face but he immediately senses his apprehension at his position of incompetence. Small comfort to Chick, Bridger shares his apprehension as all his barely relieved muscles tighten painfully. Then in an action so swift that he can hardly follow it, Chick, who has never used a bow before, plucks an arrow from his quiver, arms his weapon, and shoots, bringing down a duck that has just risen from the marsh. Satisfied, the group immediately turn their attention to individual chores, and Chick turns to him. Through those eyes, the other Chick is beaming with such pride that, for the first time, Bridger is the one amused and silently indicating approval.

With sticks and some dried moss, they get a fire going. Duck on a stick is very good, despite the distaste Bridger felt plucking the feathers and eviscerating the bird. He has done it only a couple of times before, and fully realises how spoiled he's been over many things that were once basic in everyday life. One source of gratification, though, is noticing that Chick finds it no less distasteful than he.

Around the fire, the men banter back and forth in a camaraderie not unlike any other group of men, military or otherwise. They certainly show no concern about being found by the enemy – whoever that is – although some sit apart, inspecting their arrows and testing their bows. From his spot, Bridger watches them in their after-dinner leisure, while he ponders the appalling knowledge that he really is one of them. His mind reruns again and again the moment he bent at the water's edge and saw one of these dark persons looking intently at him. Compatriot or enemy, he didn't know, but he darted away every time he swivelled around, until he finally realised this swarthy party was he. He! Brown-eyed, hawk-nosed, black-haired, with even a derelict feather bobbing from braided strands. Now, he repeatedly feels his hide clothes and studies his moccasins – these alone are not unfamiliar, although not just like any he has seen before.

Chick suddenly looms up beside him and sits down. Bridger is immediately cheered by his presence. They have little to say – so bizarre is their situation – until (seeking rationality in the trivial, perhaps) he questions the neat appearance of Chick's clothes as compared to the puckered look of his. "That's because your wife doesn't sew very well," Chick answers in a tone that says, 'you know that'. "Well," he quickly minimises at Bridger's expression, "she's just a young wife, after all."

Bridger finds it odd that he seems to be ten or twelve years younger than this Chick, although the 'real' Chick is as many years younger than the 'real' he.

That wasn't what startled him, though. It was the statement that he had a wife! An Indian wife.

He finds himself thinking of Midge. Funny, *she* couldn't sew, either.

Chick's voice draws him out of his convoluted thoughts. Chick has been listening to the camp-fire talk and now he says, "I think they expect to come upon the enemy tomorrow."

"Who is the enemy?" Bridger asks.

"I don't know, but I know we are Piegans." Chick seems just as dismayed at being a member of a different Indian nation as Bridger is at being an Indian.

In the morning, the men take things out of skin bags that they carry, and put streaks of colour on their faces. Chick draws lines on his face, and nudges Bridger. Bridger opens the bag that he has been carrying around and pulls out a menagerie of things – feathers and coloured pigment in little woven containers or wrapped in leaf. Gingerly he dabs colour here and there at Chick's instructions. As he begins putting the various articles back into the bag, one among them feels smoothly soft under his hand. He slips it away from the others. It to a flat disc of two pieces of leather placed back to back, with a thong attached to hang it from the neck. Over the dressed surface, a wildfowl, back to viewer, spreads its wings. The head is shaped somewhat so the curve can be seen. The feathers are worked in delicately to show the beautiful green head of the mallard, and a little of the white ring of the neck. The white melts away into the darkness of the wings. How has the artist been able to place the feathers so perfectly and so naturally? Though primitive in design, it is exquisite!

As he studies it, he sees the sudden picture of two shy dark eyes and two extended hands, on which lies this very talisman. Then the picture is gone and Chick is looking at him. Bridger hands him the talisman and as he inspects it the march is called.

They have met the enemy in a volley of arrows and a burst of yells his imagination has never equalled. It is a scene of stamping horses and slashing knives. Bridger has fallen from his horse at the outset and now fights from the protection of the bushes. He sees Chick unhorse a man who is aiming a blow at one of their group. The attacker, disarmed in the fall, is half up from the ground, expecting the blow of the tomahawk, but instead is grabbed by the front of his clothes and thrown clear. He lands sprawling in the bush, his black eyes showing his astonishment. He seems very young, and has no feathers in his hair.

The battle soon ends: each side gathers its wounded and retreats.

"Who are they?" Bridger asks.

"I don't know," Chick answers. "They could be Salish." A hint of self-accusation seeps into his voice at the possible irony.

When they camp for the night, there is no fire, no food. One man has strips of dried meat which he shares with another, while the rest look on. As for Bridger, he turns his face when he sees one of them stretching a scalp on a circular withe, and the pulse in his head begins to pound. Earlier he had bent at the edge of a brook and dabbed at the dried blood on his head, blood which during the battle was streaming down his face. Chick, having washed off his own wounds, came over as he puzzled at the short horizontal wound near his hairline. "You were lucky, my friend," he said. "That axe barely touched you."

Sackasack, the leader, makes demeaning remarks about people who don't venture too far from the bushes, but withdraws when Chick takes a hostile stature in defence of his friend. Bridger, without guilt, feels he has been scarred enough in this battle that isn't his anyway.

He wonders how he ever became a candidate for this group: he rides poorly and has no propensity for killing. Still he has held his own and has redeemed himself further by giving his blanket of skins and another he retrieved from the battleground to two of the seriously wounded.

He finds a little relief from this scene by watching some of the braves carefully tethering extra horses they gleaned from the battle.

"Surely we will be going home tomorrow," he questions Chick. (Where he means by "home" he doesn't know.)

"I don't think so," Chick squashes his incipient hope. "I think there are more wrongs to be avenged."

"It's a good thing we're not doing much avenging," Bridger says. "I'm useless with this bow. Rocks I'm better with."

"Have you noticed, there are no white weapons here," Chick says.

"What?"

"No *white man's* weapons. No guns. No steel knives, or hatchets. And the Piegans were the earliest in the far west to get white goods! At least this far north and away from the coast."

"Meaning?"

"Maybe this is a pre-white time."

As they shiver through the long night, Bridger thinks of two dark eyes and a talisman. "Who is she?" He asks Chick, but Chick's awareness seems not to go beyond bare knowledge. "And could, a person who does work like that, do work like this?" He asks, pulling at his tunic.

Even in the dark, Chick can see the movement. "Perhaps as a maiden she spent many moons working over that for someone – someone special," he suggests. His voice, soft in the night, seems to be caressing some memory of his own.

"Who are we?" Bridger silently questions, "here in this cool night under a white moon?"

This enemy may be slightly different, but it is the same scene of blood and yells, and horses crashing. A very big warrior swings to axe Sackasack. Bridger throws a tomahawk, which grazes the attacker, felling him. Sackasack whirls, perceives the action and bestows on him a look of commendation that leaves him tingling in his moccasins; but as Sackasack moves to finish his opponent in like manner, a breaking branch slaps his horse, causing his aim to miscarry and the enemy to escape with only wounds.

Sackasack utters some choice imprecations (Bridger can almost understand some of this language now) and Bridger casts a subtle look at Chick, who manipulated the branch.

"How long can this go on?" Bridger mumbles.

"I don't know," Chick replies wearily. "They've travelled very far and lost half their men in a few weeks."

Bridger wasn't expecting an answer to this, but he responds with the same weariness, "Every inch of my body tells me how far we've travelled. I wonder why?"

"It seems their enemies are many and distant."

"No, I mean I wonder why we're travelling with them." Bridger was again not expecting an answer, but Chick has one.

"Tnustchaen brought us here. He'll take us back when he's ready."

The grey! Bridger hasn't thought of him since – since two centuries ago. No. Two centuries ahead!

Chick is poking his arm. "There seem to be more warriors now than before," he says. "Look there!"

Through the trees, barely glimpsed forms are silently approaching on foot.

"And look over there! Chick says with fresh alarm, and points to clear ground beyond their own. "A whole bunch of them. This doesn't fall in with our strike and bolt strategy. Look at those horses!"

"I am."

"No, I mean they're different!"

"They're overwhelming!" Bridger gasps, his eyes rooted on the broad line of mounted warriors, poised and ready to dash down in a concerted assault.

"My God! Sackasack's band will be wiped out!"

The words aren't out before the line moves down the ridge in a solid wave, then breaks like foam into individual riders who sweep across the flat, disappear for a few moments at the base of the hill, then begin to show above the top of the hill, amid a horror of yells and missiles.

But what is this? They begin to fall before they are in range of Sackasack's meagre weapons. Are they fighting some other enemy? This seems to be the case, for now the onlookers can see individuals joined in close conflict with a fresher enemy that was not within their view before: and the magnitude of this battle suggests that Sackasack has infringed on two other armies. Above the clamour and the shrieks of horses, Chick's voice yells, "See that horse? That light one?"

Bewildered, Bridger shouts, "What horse? There's a whole lot of light ones!"

"That one that's fallen. He's just getting up. There! There!"

"Yes, I see."

"That's him!"

"Who?"

"The Nez Perce war horse."

"How do you know that?" Bridger gasps in amazement.

"Look at the way he moves, how he dances!"

Bridger gapes, no less bewildered. He can't see any difference in the movements – he can't even make out any one set of feet in the melee – but this isn't the resplendent horse of his memory. Any colours that once blazoned its pale coat – whether grey or buff – are now faded or corrupted to muddy streaks and splatters. The horse flings himself out of the centre of the onslaught, races down the hill, and out of sight, then reappears, only part of him showing above the crest of the hill. What is he doing, standing there in the midst of this hell while someone fumbles at his side? That's it! His fallen rider struggles on – he could be a chief. He wears a straggly cap with torn fur and remnants of feathers clinging to it, but it is long enough to once have been a fine feathered head-dress. Bridger remembers reading it was a disgrace for a chief to lose a head-dress – so a chief would hang onto it no matter what the condition. His clothes, too, are badly tattered. Everything indicates he and his army have come through some previous battle. The arrow in his breast, though, is fresh. His intent seems to be to re-enter the battle, but the horse, as though following its own wisdom, takes him away, threading through the bloody throng and into the farther woods as the rider slumps closer and closer to his supporting body.

"The grey would do that," Bridger says with admiration.

"It's not the grey," Chick says. "Could be a mare."

While this inexplicable battle rages below, the combatants of their own hostilities have melted into the safety of the forests behind. Some, though, are forced by that battle into this direction. Fully and acutely aware that they are facing their own imminent deaths, the two turn to face the shadowy forces converging on them. In his squatting position, Chick arms his bow. (It is amazing that these men can arm and fire missile after missile from this position.) Bridger picks up a rock that he has kept close, and discovers a knife someone has lost in battle. It is primitive and rough-edged, but he takes it in his hand and maintains his half-crouch. Perhaps they will work past, unnoticing.

But they are noticing. He draws his arm back to strike at one who looks very much like himself. He feels the strength of his whole body in his arm, his hand, as the knife starts its forward thrust ... into sunbeams scattering low across the dell. Somewhere chickens cluck their evening retirement, and the sweet smell of pinks fills the air. Chick, the first Chick, stands holding his horse's rope. Tnustchaen – yes, Tnustchaen – stands apart, nibbling, as always. They stand speechless and disoriented. They have travelled several hundred miles and perhaps more than two hundred years, and the sun hasn't even set!

The next morning, Bridger was awakened as Maggie and Doddie pounded down the stairs, went into the rec-room for some article, and fought over it all the way up the stairs again. Bridger got up and dressed. As he was about to start up the stairs he heard Kitty speaking from the left-open door.

"I hope Bridger's in a better mood this morning. Did you two have a fight yesterday?"

"No. What do you mean?" Arnie asked.

"He looked funny when he came in. He hardly spoke, and he went downstairs almost right away."

"Ya know, he was quiet on the way home. I think he may have got a little sun-stroke. We were out in that hot sun all day. I kept telling him to put on his hat!"

"Why didn't you tell me?" Kitty asked. "I should have gone down. Maybe he was really sick. He might still be sick."

"No, I think I heard him moving," Arnie said.

Grabbing the railing. Bridger snarled to himself, "Yes, I'm moving. And I didn't get sunstroke neither." Then the possibility jolted him. Maybe he did! Yes! A hallucination! It must have been. The heavy unreality began to lift from him. He felt better and better all day as Arnie and he worked on the fence. The steady labour, no doubt, also helped to re-establish blessed mundane reality. So well did it, that when Kitty came in all elated the next day to say that Marda had found the piece she had been looking for, he was able to be quite as excited as she.

"Marda let me borrow it," she said, taking the book out of a brown bag, "only on my oath (she stressed the word) that we return it with no pages missing, and she also gave me a little reverential book review: It was printed in 1885, and, by its title, is a collection of company and individual records to give a partial history of the trade and an intimate look into the lives of those who laboured in its employ."

Almost out of breath on that, Kitty shot a look at Bridger, then went on. "Marda says the editor stated that two of the authors of detached parts of journals cannot be identified with certainty, and in one case it cannot be determined with certainty whether the events took place before or after the amalgamation of the Norwesters and the Hudson's Bay Company.

"The *case* happens to be the papers we are concerned with, and the editor assigned it to the North West Company."

Bridger sat down at the table and began to read the yellowed leaves just as Kitty had carefully laid them open. The typical brigade tribulations unfolded as he turned the tattered pages:

"Snowbound for two weeks. Storm raged so fiercely that for three days we could not get thirty feet from camp, and Jack-knife Pete got lost. He would have died out there if some friendly Snakes had not heard his dog howling and lodged him with them until they could return him to us. Luckily, the hunters had got buffalo.

The Indians had a hard time rounding up the horses after the storm. Three were never found."

"Francois hurt his arm badly, which means he is not much use on the traps. G sent him with his party, though. Says he can stand guard – parties of hostile Indians around. LaFrambois and Gagnon complain."

The journal went on, through the seasons, through every type of terrain:

"Steep hillside, rocky ground. The horses' hooves worn to the quick. Have to fasten leather about their feet."

"The pack train jammed up ahead. Scasa rode forward on one of his fine horses to encourage them through. Scasa, a Cayuse Indian, is excellent with horses. All the Indians are – we have seventeen Indians from thirteen different tribes, in this expedition, but none of them can excel Scasa.

"One of Scasa's horses is most unusual. In appearance, drab grey with a few indistinct white spots on his rump, but he is most faithful and intelligent. M would have him, under Scasa, here and there, easing along the line, but in emergency he could press him into pack service.

"Scasa said the grey was once a highly prized buffalo horse, raised from a foal by one in his camp. It was only after he was injured that Scasa was able to acquire him in trade. His wounds must have proved slight, for he is very strong, and very swift when he cares to be."

Kitty looked over from her supper preparations as Bridger made a few exclamations, but he continued reading.

"Some of the Iroquois trappers, hired in the east, are a constant trouble. Four deserted and went to live with the local Indians. Two have returned with nothing. Their traps, their guns are lost, even the capote of one – he wears deerhide. They do not even have their horses. On leaving, they took a good horse that belonged to Gervais, who was much put out. When they returned M had to refit them at their cost: they needed everything and owed Gervais a horse.

"In the early part of the summer, one of them was able to trade an old gun to some passing Indians for a horse. It seemed not a good trade either way. This horse, given to Gervais for the one previously taken, was a very pale mare, temperamental, and she seemed not very hardy. The opposite attributes are a prime essential for brigade horses. However, during the summer she thrived and grew sturdy, and I had to admit she was a handsome horse. With her fine head and dainty step, I could see her more fittingly before a fine caleche, carrying the bourgeois at Montreal.

"The grey and the honey mare formed a strong attachment, and at the end of the day when they returned from their separate chores, they grazed always together. Indeed, the grey became resistant to being separated from her at any time.

"Such devotion, added to his other fine qualities, drew the admiration of all in the party, and he received many fond names in the different languages. But Scasa already called him something like 'Naschetsn unan'. He generally became more commonly called 'Nuja'.

"Here. This, this is like the name! Bridger exclaimed, and Kitty smiled. "This is the grey!" He looked up in excitement, then sought the page again. It went on:

"Nor was the devotion all on Nuja's part. Once when Gervais' party was returning to camp (Scasa had been sent to replace a trapper who had to be left ill at main camp), Scasa had Nuja loaded and in front of the mare in the train for the evening return. An immense piece of rock shaled away just behind the gelding. With a gasp, Gervais reached to stop the mare and detour a short distance, but she was over with the packs slapping at her sides, right behind the grey horse. 'Mon dieu!' marvelled Gervais. 'Wit de packs, she leap lak de goat!'

"As the winter came on, the mare began to lose her summer gains. Sometimes the horses are pawing through snow up to their bellies to get grass.

"Through the plains, many buffalo. At times, lots of deer and small game. But the weather grows harsher and the area poorer. I can understand M's irascible moods. Game is suddenly scarce, the people are hungry. The men complain, the poor devils are half naked in their tattered clothes.

"M sent me with two men to search out a road. We came back in three days with a possible route. Approaching camp again, we could hear some altercation on the far edge, and I stopped LaGarde as he came hurrying by. 'Bourgeois anger de mos ever see. I tink he kill dat Antoine,' he said.

"The hunters had come back with no game again, it seems, and the bourgeois had told them they'd have to kill another horse – one of those poor beasts pawing weakly at the ground.

"'Bourgeois mak fonny move when Antoine raise gun,' LaGarde continued. 'I turn lak fas an see dat pale mare on hill, an de grey look straight at Antoine, But grey more fas, take mare and dey fly up de hill, an all de horses run back an fort. Bourgeois yell "beeg fool" to Antoine. "Bes horse gone!" 'I get horse. Go fin,' LaGarde hurried on his way.

"I went over to M, who was still striding back and forth, shouting angry directions to the men saddling up again. Antoine had already streaked off in pursuit. I went back and got on my horse, which was still saddled, and searched with the men. Scasa had immediately raced out of camp, bareback as always. Though we spread out and searched thoroughly, it was soon too dark to see anything. Still, it was long later that Scasa – came dejectedly in. Though the whole camp looked out for them during the rest of our travels, we never saw either horse again."

Kitty had been watching to see him finish the account. As he did so, she said, "We should have known there was a lady horse in there. That's what the grey was looking for as he gazed over the voids with Whantoos."

"Or maybe just remembering," Bridger suggested, "since he was alone. She may simply have died. She was ailing."

"And he wandered on," Kitty guessed. "Probably allowed himself to be roped again, then traded, stolen – till he came upon someone he was willing to stay with."

"This 'bourgeois'," Bridger said, looking at the page.

"That's why they think it's the North West Company," Kitty explained before he could tender the question, "although a former Norwester might continue for a while to use that term for 'chief trader'."

"The biography of a horse," Bridger said. "We know he must have travelled up and down the tributaries of the Snake, crossed and recrossed the divide, tramped the flats, traversed the hills from the Green River drainage right up to the Columbia, his home ground: and after that wandered northward and ended up in an area of the Fraser River to become the horse of Whantoos. Kind of heady stuff, isn't it, when it all fits together?"

"Headier than just that," Kitty answered, "with his fair lady – a finely assembled lady."

"But that's irrelevant to the legend," Bridger countered the impatience in her voice.

"To the Indian legend; not to Rosalita's legend," Kitty retorted, and went on with her meal-making, perplexed at his restricted excitement.

During supper, happily, it was easy for Bridger to cling to his restrictions because Arnie would characteristically bulldoze off any introduction of subjects that courted the fantastic. Also, Kitty had had to move the book to the dining room table, thus removing it from his sight. These outward restraints couldn't last though, and later he turned the pages back till he came to the part about 'her dainty step', and 'could see her more fittingly before a fine caleche'. "See how he dances," Chick had said. "Could be a mare."

Gradually he had to admit the truth that was flooding, rather chillingly, back upon him. He hadn't dreamed that bizarre adventure. No matter how incongruously, he was involved in Nuja's quest for his pale mare.

When he ran into Chick in town the next day, he told him of their find and expected some show of excitement. Chick merely smiled. "That's our grey," he said.

"This must be the way Kitty felt yesterday," Bridger thought, and aloud said, "But what about the mare?"

"She must be the Nez Perce war horse," Chick said.

"And Rosalita's amarillo."

"What?" Chick queried.

Of course, he hadn't heard that legend. Bridger retold the story.

"Mmmhh. No, I haven't heard that one," Chick said, then added, "That's going a long way back, isn't it? And you say we string our legends to the mists of centuries! The book makes one thing certain, though," Chick said to Bridger's deflated expression. "We knew our buffalo hunter was pointing us to one special horse, which could be a mare. Now we *know* it's a mare. Well, small clue, maybe," he tacked on, wishing he hadn't so completely doused the other's spirits.

But some thought was striking across Bridger's face. "How'd you know the grey was a buffalo hunter?"

Bridger asked, his voice lifting in belated surprise. He hadn't mentioned that.

"The grey took me on a buffalo hunt," Chick answered.

"When?"

"Just a few days before he took us on the warpath. I was right there." His eyes took on the memory. "The hooves thundered and the wind raced past. The bull was just ahead, just ahead – and then it all vanished."

Bridger knew how that was and he simply nodded.

"I told Malcolm," Chick said, "and he said, 'Then it looks like responsibility for the debt has fallen on you."

"Did you tell him about the war party?" Bridger asked with interest.

"NO. Well, it became too intricate," Chick excused the omission. "Astounding relationships!"

"Yes," Bridger agreed, "Astounding!"

CHAPTER FOUR

The next day Arnie had another schedule of business laid out. Bridger didn't really want to go with him, but Arnie insisted. That meant a whole day of going here and going there.

Rillas escorted them out if the last of the barns, where they had seen some of his fine horses. They crossed the narrow end of the paved concourse that linked the house to the barns. Going on from the last barn – for miles, it looked – was a line of lombardy poplars and a fence that sliced right down the middle of the land. In front of them, the land was cut off into fenced fields of different sizes: they lay along the edge of the pavement, and in the L of the concourse was a riding ring. More horses grazed, separated into various fields close and far.

"And here's your Blackmire," Rillas said.

Alone in a small field directly in front of them, Blackmire, a sprightly youngster that showed, apparently, all the qualities that Rillas required, raced up to the fence for some admiring attention. Arnie was pleased, for he had sold him the colt a year ago. He would have lingered longer, but Rillas urged them on.

"C'mon," he said, leading them to the riding ring, where a young man was taking a horse over the jumps. "I want you to see Chieftain's Queen! She's our star performer. What do you think of her?"

What a beautiful animal she was: pure white, the body trim and smoothly slender, head high and haughty. The white mane feathered up, the forelegs synchronised into graceful curls as she took the jumps one after the other.

While Rillas clucked, both Arnie and Bridger made sounds of genuine admiration.

"Louise's little filly turned out a real Cinderella, didn't she?" Arnie observed.

"She did," Rillas admitted cheerfully. "She's got it all!"

"Even the name," Bridger interjected.

"Oh," Arnie said – it took him a few seconds to understand "Nearly all Rillas' horses are 'Queens'."

"Yes," Rillas turned at the statement. "I have a weakness for 'Queens', I have to admit. That's Gypsy Queen over there, and away over, that black mare is Queen of the Niger."

"How does he get so many excellent horses?" Bridger asked, after they had left.

"Oh he's got an eye for them. And the money," Arnie said. "He can't take the credit for Snow, though."

"Snow?"

"The one he calls Chieftain's Queen. He bought her for his daughter – she was only fourteen or fifteen at the time. That was about ten years ago. He sure didn't want to, but his wife insisted when she realised that Louise wanted that horse and no other. It had all the papers," Arnie went on, "but it was small. It seemed frail, but it wasn't really. That was one time Rillas didn't have an eye for the right horse. It was slow, though. Louise, in a few years, put her into minor jumping. It was only two years ago that Rillas realised her ability, and persuaded, I should say 'harassed', Louise to put her into competition. Louise really didn't want to."

Arnie had two pieces of business in Chilliwack and Veddar. Somewhere up there as they went back and forth they had some chicken, which Bridger thought was very good: then the next thing he knew, they were riding along a forested road. Presently where the road curved around, Arnie slowed, then pulled over and stopped at an open spot that overlooked the whole valley.

"Rillas' place is right down there," he said. "There's the road we went in from before."

It was a luxurious spread. The house meandered off into limbs – off one limb was the concourse they had walked. The lombardy poplars and the barns now backed the field that lay against the mountain. There was a riding ring on this side, too. It had access to the back area of the concourse, and it could be viewed from the room, or rooms, behind that curved wall of windows.

Rillas had mentioned that they preferred this ring, but that Chieftain's Queen seemed agitated lately. "There's a stray up there on the hill," he had said, "but I can never find it when I get up there."

That was just the west wing; around the east wing, trees and shrubs grew in just the right places. Flowers bloomed in rockeries and plots, in borders, beside little bridges, and up the sides of rock-built steps that led to tennis courts and a swimming pool. To complete the perfection, beautiful horses grazed on fields that looked as though they had been mowed.

Away off on the other side of the poplars, the white horse raced up and down the field, flinging her head and charging off. Closer was Gypsy Queen. She was a beauty, too – long white mane and tail ('points' Arnie said), high head, prancing step that took her toward the hill, then danced her to a stop while she eyed the rising landscape.

"They sure are pretty," Bridger had to say again, looking to Arnie.

He agreed with a nod of his head, and then said, "They do seem agitated. Must be other horses close."

Bridger couldn't see where, but as they rolled on and began to descend the less rugged end of the hill, they did see horses in the fenced corner of the next property.

"See," Arnie said, "his neighbour's land extends back with the curve of the mountain."

"Yeah, I see," Bridger agreed, looking back. Through the thinned-out cover, he could see something – something light against the leaves – standing there stolidly, looking down on the field.

"Nuja," he mumbled.

"What?" Arnie asked.

"Chick's grey horse."

Arnie laughed. "You've got that horse on the brain."

"No," he protested, but the picture was wrenched away from him as the car proceeded down onto the flats and into the blinding rays of the low sun. All the way home with his hat pulled low against the sinking ball of fire, he thought, "He must be right. It was just lighter foliage."

The next day, however, he couldn't help but ask Arnie, "You know that horse we saw yesterday, Gypsy Queen? What colour is she?"

"Well, Rillas calls her a palomino," Arnie answered.

"But she's not all pale."

"No, she's kind of brownish. Some would call her a light sorrel."

"But what would you call her?" Bridger persisted.

"Oh one of those," Arnie answered infuriatingly, as he walked off to the barn.

"I'd call her yellow," Bridger said to himself.

Bridger kept expecting to run into Chick in town the next day (for that's the way it always seemed to follow), but he didn't. On the following day he asked Kitty if she knew how to get in touch with him or his relatives.

"Gee, I don't," she said. "I think Malcolm lives in Sumas. No, Chilliwack. No – Arnie could tell you when he gets home."

"Don't let him know!" Bridger said hastily.

Kitty had answered his query a little dubiously, and at his reaction to mention of Arnie she said, "Bridger, are you getting a little too serious about this Indian legend?"

"No," he answered. "I've got to let Chick know where Nuja is. Come on, Kitty, you're the one who eagerly helped me search out the threads of this legend."

"That's what I mean. We searched out Nuja's history, but that took place nearly two hundred years ago. This horse isn't Nuja. Sometimes I think you get mesmerised by Chick's thinking."

"Oh yes? Who was the one reaching for Rosalita's tale to weave a well-built mare into the legend?"

"Just a fun fantasy," she emphasised.

"Well the fun has run out of this fantasy," he retorted a little harshly. "I've got to tell Chick that Nuja – okay, the grey – is up above Rillas' place, looking over his mares."

That jolted Kitty. "The scrub? Rillas will kill him!"

"This is real enough, then, to merit finding Chick?"

"Yes! I'll look through Arnie's stuff and see if I can find a number."

After much waiting Bridger was finally connected with Chick, who was much astonished at his call and then rather dubious about the message, but he agreed to meet them. At the designated spot, he was already waiting when they drove up in Kitty's car, and he followed in his truck. At the overview spot, they got out of their vehicles and looked down on the gracious scene.

"Look at those horses!" Chick said, deeply impressed.

"They are gorgeous," Kitty agreed.

Every horse seemed prompted to put on its most graceful performance. The black mare and a chestnut raced each other in one field. Gypsy Queen had been lying down. She pushed up on her forelegs, then heaved her rump up, shook herself, did a trial turn in one direction, then doubled back with fancy step towards two other cavorting horses at the end of her pasture. The white mare, alone in her turf, took step with two others racing in the adjoining field. Halfway down, they were returning. She danced to a stop, flung her head, and took after them, gathering speed with beautiful motions.

Even from this unequalled viewing post, Bridger doubted that Chick could discriminate one very particular horse from these beauties, but he did.

"That's her," he said with that absolute surety with which he had once before identified her.

"The white?" Bridger asked, and Chick nodded.

"Her who?" Kitty asked, puzzled.

"The Nez Perce war horse," Chick inflected in that 'you know what I'm talking about' tone.

But, of course, Kitty hadn't known. She was incredulous. "Snow? Snow is the Nez Perce war horse! That's ridiculous!"

Chick was a little taken aback by the explosive outburst. "Well, in a time long ago she was a Nez Perce war horse," he said, but his attention was already swinging back to the scene below.

"I think I've seen that horse before! I mean recently. I mean *now* recently," he spluttered in the ambiguity of his observations.

"She's been doing well in the jumps," Kitty said, "locally in the west and across the border. She's got all summer to go. A couple of international horse shows and a derby or two."

"That's right!" Chick said with quick enthusiasm. "My uncle's been following her rising star. Snow? That doesn't seem to..."

"Chieftain's Queen," Kitty put in. "Rillas registered her in that name, but Louise has always called her Snow."

Chick studied the horse further, then said, "So you intend to take her away, Tnustchaen."

As Kitty and Bridger cast enquiring eyes on him at his direct address to a missing horse, he pointed. "There he is! His rump stands out clearly there. Follow the lighter colour behind the branches. See his head?"

Oh! .Yes. There he was, gazing steadily on the field, paying absolutely no attention to the voices above. In a moment Chick turned to leave.

"You can't just let him take her away," Kitty protested.

"I can't stop him, when he decides the time," Chick said. "We'll just have to wait and watch for his move. He's not my horse; he's my creditor."

"This doesn't make sense," Bridger said as they made a movement toward their vehicles. "The grey found his mare by himself! He didn't need us. Why was he giving us those obscure clues?"

"The grey works in mysterious ways," Chick answered. "Maybe he needs us to get her out."

He turned back. "Yes, you steered us here," he said, "but Snow has a commitment first. You understand that."

He spoke as though there was this reciprocal sense of obligation between them. Perhaps there was, but, in only a few days, Chick would attempt to impose a measure of restraint on the grey as he grew slightly impatient with the demands of man's world.

When the day came, Chick sought out Bridger and they made their way down the thickly forested mountainside. The grey made no acknowledgement of their presence as they picked their way down, until they were within three feet of him. Then be turned those unflinching eyes on them, and they knew to go no closer; at least Bridger did. Chick dared to approach slowly, and even to lay his hand on the grey's neck. "It demands time," he said. "I guess you know that better than I do."

The horse seemed to be reluctantly acquiescing, then suddenly made a movement. Bridger plunged to the safety of a big cedar, but Chick, with no place to go, and his hand already on the mane, grabbed it and leaped onto his back. The grey slashed around like a whirlwind caught in the thick growth, dodging low branches and whipping against lower bush.

"My God!" Bridger thought. "He'll be killed!"

Chick stayed on, draped over the grey's body like a coat, his boots digging into the girth, and his hands clinging to the loose flesh of the neck. He spoke quick words in the Indian tongue. Finally the grey slowed his frantic motions, then stopped. Chick slid off and slumped to the ground.

Weak with relief, Bridger made his way over to him.

"How did you do that?" he asked. "I thought he'd kill you!"

"I thought he would, too," Chick said, sitting up. "But I guess he wasn't intending that, or he could have, easily. I think he's impressing on me that if he has to wait, he isn't doing it with respectful patience."

"What language were you speaking, Salish or Blackfoot?" "Salish. I don't know much Blackfoot, now."

Bridger knew that. He just wondered if Chick was remembering. In a few minutes, Chick pushed himself up. "We might as well go," he said. "God, I feel like a scrambled egg."

"The grey?" Bridger queried. The grey stood there stolidly, his eyes rooted on the field.

"He won't do anything," Chick said. "He's just keeping his watch."

CHAPTER FIVE

In the ring, the horses jerked and resisted; the youngsters demanded and pleaded. It was serious practice (the first for some), readying for this competition; the horses new to this, reacting incorrectly to commands; the young masters expending great energy just to cajole an equine foot two inches to the right. Louise laughed at her young brother's look of exasperation.

"C'mon, Kenny, this is only practice tonight. Tomorrow is the real thing."

As she stood at the rail she heard her father's voice speaking excitedly (as was usual these days).

"Louise! There you are! I brought the English saddle. Louise, I found out who owns that coyote of a nag that's been up above the house the last while. It belongs to that Indian. There he is!"

"Indian?" Louise turned to him.

"Yes. He's related to Malcolm. Name's Chick. You may remember him from years ago. I'm going to talk to him."

Louise looked calmly at the figure paused momentarily in the big doorway between barns. "He grew up nice-looking, didn't he?"

Rillas slammed the saddle into her arms. "Here!" he crackled at her irrelevant rejoinder, and raced after the retreating form. The first day of the show was taken with mostly horse and cart. At one point, Rillas came in railing about 'that damn Arnie' as Louise helped her brother and some of her students to harness their horses.

"Arnie! Arnie Derkson?" She asked.

"Yeah."

"What's he got to do with it?"

"Oh, he's out there with Chick and Malcolm, making dumb remarks."

"Well, if Arnie's in on it, you know it's just a joke."

"Are you saying I haven't seen that horse up there?"

"I'm saying I think you're uptight about Snow and how she's going to perform for the next six weeks. Why don't you simmer down?"

"Simmer down! Sim..." Rillas realised a dozen twelve to fourteen-year olds were watching him with glee, and he whirled around and hurried off.

The next day, the youngsters were dressed in their finest western garb: boots were polished, saddles were rubbed to their finest lustre.

"If we can just get through this show without Dad running into Malcolm," Louise thought.

But no, there were the sounds of her father's voice, wafting even through all the rain, into the showbarn.

"Get that other halter onto Babs," she said to her young brother. "I'll be back in a few minutes."

Outside, Rillas had cornered Malcolm and Chick, and also Arnie, who, like Malcolm, had been in and out aiding his son. The situation apparently wasn't so eruptive as it sounded inside. Malcolm and Arnie were still in possession of their good nature, and the darkly handsome Chick was handling the verbal assault with control. But who was the other good-looking man saying nothing, but obviously a part of the group?

As she made a few steps into the rain, her father ended his tirade and stalked off towards his truck. The others hurried off to another entrance. None of them saw Louise, who turned back.

She was immediately taken up again in her students' preparations to get onto the floor, but as the show progressed, she had time for long glances at the 'group of four'. They weren't really together now. Chick and Malcolm were together, watching Malcolm's son. He had a good horse, and throughout the day he was to handle it well. A short distance away Arnie and the stranger watched with Gus as their focal point. She could see Arnie making remarks and his hands making motions, while the other man nodded. Gus was to have difficulties all day, on the horse or off. In the halter class, the horse wouldn't come up to the position of the other horses, then it wouldn't back up straight, and took a stoic stand angled to the others. Louise could see the smile on the face of the other man at this, while Arnie shook his head.

Although she usually ran into Arnie dozens of times on these occasions, their paths seemed destined not to cross today . When she went for coffee, he and his friend were headed back to the stands or the stabling area. Lunch break was spent seeing that horses and ruptured dispositions were separated, while Kenny went for hamburgers.

As the show started again, her father arrived.

"Where have you been?" she asked irritably. "You promised to help some."

"I couldn't get back any sooner, Louise," he replied in like tone. "How's he doing?"

"Oh so-so. Malcolm's son is taking a lot of ribbons. Arnie's son isn't doing so well, though."

"Mmh. Yeah, I see Arnie and his brother up there."

"Brother?" Louise looked up at tank-sized Arnie, and the slim man beside him.

Rillas followed her look. "Yeah, that's his brother."

"All the years we've known Arnie," she thought, "and I didn't know he had a brother like that."

Two days later, Louise went with her father to an auction barn. As she came out into the sunshine, which had returned after a sodden weekend, she saw Arnie and his brother again. Arnie was holding forth to a third party while his brother looked on.

Seated in the top rail of a fence, one foot on a bale of hay, he looked so trim and agile, you could almost see him swinging into a saddle. Yet he couldn't even ride a horse – so they kept saying. 'They' being just about everybody else (who all spoke familiarly of him). Where had she been the last few months? And, naturally, there they went, taking off just as she was about to meander over. Well, since all contrived coincidences repeatedly failed, she would have to be more forthright. The next day she drove into Derksons'.

"Louise!" Kitty said. "Haven't seen you in ages. Just in time for coffee."

"I brought Arnie that big punch Dad said he'd lend him."

"Oh," Kitty said, taking it. "I don't think he needs it right now."

"I was passing anyway. I told Dad I'd drop it off." Two days later she dropped off two nice halter buckles Arnie had once eyed covetously, as her father stashed them away in a drawer.

"Why didn't Rillas send me these buckles three months ago?" Arnie remarked later. "I could have put them on St. John's halter."

Kitty looked over with a little snort, "I don't think he volunteered them, but I'm sure Louise would have brought them three months ago if she had known Bridge was here."

"Yeah," Arnie rubbed one of the buckles on his sleeve and held it up to admire the shine. "She's really trying to rope him, but he's shying away pretty nimbly!"

"Ha! ha!" Kitty articulated deliberately at the sentiment of his male ego. "He likes her. She's coming to the meet Saturday."

"I hope her father's not coming! All we'll hear about is that grey scrub!"

"Rillas won't come *there*," Kitty said. "And anyway, Richard is leaving in the next day or two with Snow and the black on circuit."

"What difference does that make? If there's a stray horse up there, it'll still be there."

"Not if Snow's not there."

"Ooph," Arnie scoffed. "You and Bridge with your all-knowing *horse*, of all things!"

"Well why not a horse?" Kitty replied. "Six million years of the horse might suggest a long seniority in prescience."

After a minute of apparently thinking about the horse, Arnie said, "I still don't know why Rillas doesn't put a rope on that horse and take him to the pound, although he said he couldn't get a rope on him in that bush even if he could keep him in sight." Arnie didn't know that Chick, exasperated with Rillas' continued nagging, and Arnie's

74

ridiculous suggestions the previous weekend, had already intervened with his visit to the grey.

Arnie thought he was finally going to get away for coffee, but Kitty's voice stopped him.

"Tracker's doing it again. You'd better stay with Gus; he won't be able to control him. I've got the two little kids and Maggie's pony to handle."

"I'll go bring back coffee," Bridger said.

"I'll go with you." Louise joined him quickly.

When they got to the nearest coffee shack, they found the coffee had run out and the new brew was not yet ready.

"We'll have to go to the cafeteria in the barn," Louise said.

They passed through the forward end of the barn, and the office area. On a wall, which everyone passed going to the stands, was a huge poster, a lovely close-up of a pretty blonde girl, dressed from hat to boots in white westerns, and seated on a white horse. A single branch of apple blossom hung above her shoulder. Bridger stopped to gaze at it.

"That's me," Louise said.

"I know, I recognised you."

"That was part of a promotional advertisement put out collectively last year by several Fraser Valley Equestrian groups."

"Mm. That must be Snow," he said of the horse.

"Yes, it is... You don't like it," she said to his seemingly negative perusal.

"Yes I do," he contradicted. "I like it and I like the white motif, too."

"But?" she pressed.

"No buts. Now that the picture has done its job. it suggests another. I'd step you and the horse back in the frame, and I'd make it winter. You'd have a smaller hat with a flatter brim to enhance the charm of that face, rather than overwhelm it. You'd need a winter jacket instead of that waist-hugger – finished in the same soft leather, though. It would hang loose so the bottom edges would fall on the black saddle. And showing from the unbuttoned lapels would be a soft woollen scarf, threaded with silver. All around you the ice would be shining – on trees and on blades of grass; and I'd caption you 'Ice Queen'."

A wave of pleasure surged over her at this, surely sincere, compliment, rendering her, for an unusual moment, speechless.

"Are you in advertising? A photographer?" she asked when speech returned, not knowing how to receive such an accolade.

"No-o," he laughed. "I worked in market trends and statistics. I used to draw, though. Just black and white. I illustrated for a little magazine for a few years, till it went broke. My drawing, maybe," he finished jokingly.

Later in the day they found themselves by the rail at the time the chariots took their run; big equipment working in a neighbouring field started up again at the same time. The machinery cranked loudly, the chariots rolled raucously, and the onlookers yelled to hear each other.

"That looks even harder than hanging onto a horse," Bridger said with admiration.

"You could ride," Louise shouted back. He shook his head negatively.

"Come up to my place. There's lots of empty trails," she urged.

"No."

"Then I'll come down to your place and you choose Arnie's most docile horse."

"No. I mean you can come down, but no horses."

"C'mon." Her head tilted in a laugh. "You can learn to ride."

"No, I can't," he said as the equipment screeched. "I haven't learned in over two hundred years."

"What?" she asked against the relentless din.

"We sure owe something to Bridge," Kitty said as she looked from the window. Over on the riding ring, she could see Gus and Maggie circling under Louise's instruction. To a command Kitty couldn't hear, they stopped their horses (not with their complete co-operation) and turned to proceed in the other direction.

"Yeah," Arnie said as he put pieces of hardware into a box. "He won't get on a horse – well, we've only got him on once or twice, ourselves – so she has to give the kids lessons to get close to him. Guess he's got something going for him."

"Well, of course he's got something going for him," Kitty laughed. "He's very attractive."

"Attractive?"

"Yes. Tall, nice grey eyes, tawny hair." Kitty shot him a glance. "But of course not as attractive as you with those blue eyes and dark curly locks," she teased.

"Uh huh," Arnie accepted the message.

"Anyway, I appreciate it," Kitty went on. "You haven't done much with the kids this year."

"Well, I've been all my time with Bridge, you know."

"I know. I don't mean it that way. Where are you going?" she asked, as he picked up the box and started across the floor.

"I have to go in and change some of these pipe joinings. See you later."

From the rail Bridger looked up as the door banged. He waved, as Arnie went down the steps, then turned back to observe the lesson.

"Don't wander off like that, Maggie. Pull your left rein, and get your reins the same length. Slap your right foot against his side!"

This had been going on for some time, with the pony best man. However, he began to move more willingly to the pressure, and Bridger realised he had been pressing the fingers of one hand hard against his palm, as if clinging to the mane of a free-moving horse. Maggie had been almost in tears earlier; now in the pose of her body, she showed she had gained a degree of confidence.

Bridger turned his eyes on Louise. "She's pretty good," he thought, as she called the speeds.

"Gus, slow it down and change lead." On they went around. "One more time and bring them up facing me. I want you to practise backing."

As they started the last lap, she looked at Bridger, who (she had been pleasurably aware) was observing her intently. She expected some relevant remark, but he asked, "Can you sew?"

"Sew?"

"I mean, sew well?"

"I sew. I think I sew well. Why? Have you got some clothes that are falling apart?"

"No. I just wondered."

Louise turned puzzled eyes back to the track, as the two riders came up. "Okay, space yourselves. Lots of room."

Louise pulled her boots off at the door.

"Lesson over for today?" Kitty asked.

"Yeah. I've got them all out there brushing down their horses. Even Doddie's doing a few strokes. I got him on the pony earlier today."

"I saw it," Kitty admitted. I thought I'd better not go down."

"It was touch and go," Louise admitted.

"Doddie's like Bridge," Kitty said. "He doesn't want to get on a horse."

"That's probably why Bridge isn't here today," Louise was prompted to say. "His hands clench tight, as though he himself is holding on for dear life.

Kitty laughed heartily. "Well, as we've noted, Bridge has no rapport with horses – although he has a kind of communication with one."

"Communication?" Louise arched an eyebrow. That sounds like something Bridge would say."

"What do you mean?"

"He says funny things." Louise went on as Kitty seemed momentarily out of words, "By 'one', I presume you mean that grey Indian legend in the flesh. They say that just about every year. I haven't seen this year's grey horse."

"No, but your dad has."

"Oh you're in on the joke, too?"

"Joke?"

"Yes. Taking advantage of this stray horse to kid my dad. He asks for it, I know. Flying off at everybody! But it is making his nerves ragged. Well, it's eased off now. The stray hasn't been around lately."

"Not since Snow left with Richard," Kitty said.

"There you go again. Still kidding."

Kitty looked a little hurt. "Well, Arnie's kidding, but the others aren't," Kitty said. "I'm not."

"Oh, yes, the grey, came looking for Snow," Louise said mockingly. "Once they were pack horses."

"Oh, then Bridger's told you about the journal," Kitty said.

"Uh huh. I wish he'd talk of something serious once in a while."

"Oh, like what?"

"Like himself – or us."

"Well, he's only known you a short while," Kitty said, glad of the change of subject. "Give him time."

"No, it's not that. I know he likes me. It's just that he seems very careful not to talk about anything that could be the least bit serious."

"A defensive tactic," Kitty said.

Louise looked directly at her. "I know he was divorced, and I can understand him avoiding involvement."

"Mm, well. I couldn't comment on that," Kitty said after a moment of silence.

"Sometimes I think it's the money. I mean," she said to Kitty's quizzical glance, "maybe he thinks if he's eager, I'd think he was interested in me because my father's rich."

"That's a thought-twister," Kitty answered. "Anyway, I doubt it. His father-in-law – ex-father-in-law – is filthy rich, and Bridger was never intimidated by his money. Anyway, Bridge has enough money of his own not to worry. Midge made them lots on the stock market. That's not his problem."

Immediately she realised she had made a slip, and Louise seized on it.

"What is his problem then?"

Kitty fell into a frustrated silence.

"He's a solitary drinker, isn't he?"

"Where'd you get that idea?" Kitty almost gasped.

"Some say they've seen him drinking all by himself."

"Oh that was early in the spring, when Arnie dragged him all over to those practices. He found it so cold! He drank coffee, too, you know. Besides, Arnie drinks more than Bridge does."

"But some people become alcoholics quicker. He might need intensive support right now!"

"He isn't drinking now," Kitty said, startled at the intent of the statement. "Would you take a situation like that on yourself?"

"If it goes with *him*, yes." Her voice was intense.

"How can you feel that way?" Kitty asked in disbelief. "You've only known him three weeks!"

"I know. It's strange. I've fallen head over heels before, but this is different."

"Strange she'd say 'strange'," Kitty thought.

"I mean it, Kitty," Louise went on, misreading her gaze as disapproval. "No matter what problem he's got."

"He's got multiple sclerosis," Kitty answered. "He was even in the hospital a while, two years ago. He was back to work a couple of times, and he moved to an apartment nearer a place where he took therapy. When Midge came back from Hong Kong, she and her father wanted to send him to a clinic in Europe, but he resisted that. He was improving. It was depression mostly he was suffering.

"That's when Arnie went out and brought him back here. He thought a different environment might help. You know – it was all offices and computers – a business world. Arnie thought he'd put him to handling animals that were big and pushed back. The doctors said to go ahead, try everything.

"He came out here just before Christmas. In the winter, Arnie made him shovel manure and toss hay. In the spring he dragged him to every practice and tune-up meet he heard of just so he could make him handle the horses. He didn't really let him sit too long, by himself. Bridger tended to try to duck away, but the weather was so cold and damp he'd be forced to participate in the handling – if not the riding – and he didn't take it all kindly. Don't think he hasn't got a temper!

"Despite all that, we like to think Arnie's therapy has worked. He's got almost complete flexibility in his hands now. The truth probably is that the disease just went into remission by itself."

Louise had sat, pathetically stunned. "My parents had a friend who died of that," she said. "I remember his wife doing so much for him, and then he couldn't get out of bed. I thought he was old – I was just a kid at the time – but he was hardly much older than Bridge is now."

With a pang of sympathy, Kitty said, "That's an extreme case. Some live into old age with it. Some don't get any worse. I know others who have had it for a long time. He might not have an attack as serious as that again."

A slight lightening of expression showed on the girl's face.

Kitty was relieved and heartened. "I hope you won't mention this to him," she said. "He doesn't like... you know now why he avoids any serious talk."

CHAPTER SIX

"I gave them a really stiff practice today. That should be good for the playday, Sunday," Louise said as she came and sat down by Bridger on the back steps. He knew she was going to Alberta for a week to help Richard with the two horses; Richard's friend, taking advantage of the proximity to relatives, was taking time off to visit.

Bridger nodded but remained silent.

"What are you thinking?" she asked.

"I was wondering," he said, "if you ever get tired of working with horses; travelling with horses; up there with your classes; down here with these kids?"

She merely grinned and shook her head.

"How come you don't ride Snow in these things yourself?" He pursued.

"Oh, no," she was quick to answer. "This is really Dad's show. If Richard hadn't agreed to ride her, he'd have been out of luck. She's too hard to handle now. When she was younger and I was younger, we both liked a good run. No longer. Now I just like doing what I'm doing, and Snow likes doing what she feels like."

Bridger looked off across the field. "I'd like to get in a car and go where there are no horses – just for a while. Maybe to a beach or a river – sit on the bank and watch the river go by."

"Is that what you used to do when..."

"No," he anticipated her question. "Midge wasn't a 'river bank' kind of person. She had us running to theatres and plays and concerts. Tennis. She liked tennis – and business. Midge loved business confabs, business trips. I didn't realise it at the time, but that's when I caught my breath, when she left on business trips. I thought I was half the energy, but she carried me."

"And what did *you* like when you were catching your breath?"

Bridger thought about it for a few moments, then answered, "I used to like everything. I liked doing what she did then. I liked catching my breath at reading or walking, or goofing around with Mackie. Life was an exciting place to be. Things change."

Trying to steer the conversation to happier thoughts, Louise asked, "Who's Mackie?"

"A friend. He got divorced too, in the usual amicable way. And then – it was unfair – things change again."

Arnie came to the doorway at that moment. "Karley's just phoned. He's got an emergency. C'mon Bridge, I need ya," he said, starting down the steps.

With a word to Louise, Bridger got up and joined him, and Louise went into the house to say goodbye to Kitty. She took a freshly-baked cookie – exclaiming how good it was – and walked to the dining-room. She stood at the table there, looking down at the white paper.

It was barely a week ago that she had taken a pencil from her purse and handed it to Bridger.

"You said you needed a soft pencil to draw," she had said at his perplexed look. "Here's some paper." She had pulled over some loose leaf sheets that lay on the table.

"It's lined!"

"So! Can't you draw on lined paper?"

Kitty, hearing this, had come to the door of the room. It had never occurred to her or to Arnie to place drawing equipment in front of Bridger. He had sat down and made timid strokes on the paper, bit soon the lines had grown bolder.

"Gus has some typing paper in his room," Kitty had said with a touch of excitement.

In just a few days he was sketching faces they could recognise.

"That's my pony," Maggie said.

"Yes," Kitty agreed.

"That's his latest," Kitty said now, from the kitchen. It was a broad view, sketchy indeed, but it was clear, a grassy scene. Grass took all the foreground and stretched up a moderate rise; a line of small trees stretched along the horizon beyond the crest of the rise, and an old stump stood at its foot; the grass planed away past the stump and into what looked like water – the edge of a lake. Two horses stood in the picture, one on the rise, its head uplifted in a suggestion of haughtiness. It was white – at any rate, pale, since the sketch was black and white. The other, darker, stood nearer the lake. Its head was bent to the ground in the munching posture so typical of the inimitable grey.

"Are you drawing on Bridger's picture!" Kitty exclaimed as she looked in to see Louise making busy marks on the sheet. "He'll kill you!"

"No. It needed that," Louise said, unconcerned.

"I've got to go," she added, putting the pencil down. "Tell Bridge I'll see him tonight."

"What?" Bridger retorted as Kitty told him later. Then he laughed. "Well, couldn't hurt it much."

It was after supper before he passed through the dining room, and stopped to look at his doctored sketch. He had spent some effort setting his scene. He had moved the stump several times. To the right. To the rise. Back down.

Displacing some of the grass, Louise had put in a small bush in blossom – you could tell those little curls were blossoms. He smiled – she could sketch, too. Yes, it was just like that, the little bush, the grass reaching to the lake, sometimes the horses. He could smell the spring air, it was so real! But where? Where was it just like that? And how did *she* know?

When Louise arrived later, she immediately started to laugh as he pointed to the table.

"I'm sorry," she giggled. "I shouldn't have done that. After I left I realised I shouldn't have done that."

He started to say, "How did you know," then changed the words to, "How come you did that?"

"I don't know! It was just an impulse. Can't you erase it?"

"No. No, it's – I like it there. It doesn't matter," he said, dismissing the whole thing as amusing, and firmly ending it.

They were winning lots of ribbons in this playday.

"Gus is handling well, and did you see Maggie do that pole-bending? Pretty smooth, aye?" Kitty remarked, and Bridger nodded.

"I hope they'll do as well next Saturday," she went on. "Probably not, though. They'll fall back, with Louise away all week."

Bridger helped put the saddles on, helped tether the horses. He saddled Arnie's favourite, big St. John. Arnie looked surreptitiously on to see the blanket was smooth, the cinch tight: then he inserted three fingers under the saddle strap anyway. Bridger had even got the bit in easily this time. Arnie threw the reins up and mounted to a groaning of leather. Bridger was sure the horse looked pained, but he got a 'first' and a 'second' in the flat races. Even Kitty's lovable Pinjam lolloped in for two ribbons.

Bridger moved the horses from place to place: put Pinjam in a sleepy corner, moved St. John away from grass.

"Pretending I'm really nonchalant and all," he said as he caught Kitty's gaze on him, "and all the time I think they're going to bite me in the head."

"You're doing fine, Bridge," Kitty smiled her lovely smile. She was tough-framed and beautiful, called 'Kitty', some thought, not after pussycat, but after mountain cat. Actually, her name was simply short for Kittson.

"Gosh, there're more horses here than kids," Arnie said, and walked over shouting instructions to Gus. Tracker had backed up ten feet before Gus got him stopped. Kitty and Bridger stood watching.

"Look at that!" Kitty said. "And last week he was good as gold. I hope Louise comes. She's better with Gus than Arnie is. She levels more discipline and less yell. She was pretty tired last night, though, after just getting home."

"She said she'd be here, though," Bridger answered. "Here she comes now!"

Louise came up on the run. "I'm sorry. I meant to be here early, but I slept in. I see Gus and Tracker are contesting each other already."

"Yes, I can handle Maggie and her pony if you get to Gus," Kitty said.

"Okay," Louise took a flat object from her jacket and pressed it into Bridger's hand as she hurried to Gus.

"What is it?"

"You asked if I could sew," she flung back.

"A picture?" Bridger asked.

Kitty bent close over it. "She's done that in needle-point," she said after scrutinising it. "That's lovely. The feathers over the back look absolutely real!"

She stepped away to assist Maggie, leaving Bridger fumbling at the plastic casing. Finally the little rectangle of cloth was freed. The head, the bit of foot tucked under the body, and the wing of a little yellow bird were done in petit point, but on the back and the breast, both eye and thumb descried real feathers, perfectly and continuously set in. It was exquisite!

A few moments later when Louise came back, he was still studying the little piece of cloth.

"Do I pass the test?" she asked.

"Test?"

"The bird. Do I sew well enough?"

"Beautifully," he said, realising what she meant. "How did you get these feathers in so perfectly?"

"Ahh," she said, leaving it at that, but a moment later when Kitty asked her the same question, she was willing to go into detail with another woman.

"Oh, Trish and I were fooling around with them one year. She had a big bag of moulted budgie feathers. We tried to work them into a pair of pictures we did for her mother – her club was holding a bazaar. We were spectacularly unsuccessful, but later I started working on them independently. I don't know why I took such an interest in using feathers, or how I stayed with it. I'd get so frustrated I'd throw everything in the drawer and swear I'd never touch it again. Then I'd come back to it. With a few tips from a friend of mine who worked in a hobby shop, I came up with a process of gluing them. By that time most of the feathers were ruined, but I managed to salvage enough yellow ones. It took two years to find the way, but it turned out well, so well that Trish wanted me to enter it in one of the fairs. Do you know, she got three firsts on her petit point and cross-stitch! She does beautiful work."

"*This* is beautiful," Kitty said. "You should have entered it."

"No. When I finished it I wrapped it away in the drawer. It was too small for the dresser-set trio I was doing, and it didn't go well with any combination of others. It seemed to want to be by itself in some special niche."

Neither of them noticed the expression on Bridger's face.

Louise turned to Maggie, who was tugging at her for some instruction, and Kitty called to Arnie, who came over, looked, said "Yeah, nice," and walked back to the person he'd been conversing with. At Kitty's shout, another bystander had moved close on a horse. Bridger looked up to see Chick peering curiously down. Silently Bridger handed him the little rectangle of cloth. Chick studied it closely and drew his thumb over the feathered back. "Where'd you get it?" He asked.

"From Louise."

Chick's keen dark eyes moved from Bridger to the girl bending over Maggie, then back again. In his penetrating glance, Bridger could read his own thoughts; then Chick nudged Chase away.

Bridger put the little picture back in its plastic case, but Louise noticed him looking at it often during the day.

"I think I've finally made a hit," she said at one point. "You like that bird so much. The case is made to go on the outside of your wallet. If it doesn't fit your wallet, I just happen to have one at home that it does."

As he smiled at that she went on, "And to think I fought with myself about giving it to you. I kept telling myself I should make you a shirt."

"No! No. I like this bird," he said with an intensity that pleased her.

"Since you do, and since with Richard arriving home Monday, I'm taking Tuesday off, do you think Arnie can do without you for a day, and I'll take you to some remote, seductive spot by a lazy river?"

The river ran softly by, so slowly it seemed hardly to be moving. Fallen leaves floated like sleeping ducks in a shore-side eddy. The day itself was as quiet and soft as the current; sunshine laced through the trees and birds twittered in low peaceable notes.

Louise packed up some of the leftover picnic articles, and Bridger came back from the stream with the rinsed cups, then sat down, but apparently on his wallet, for he took it from his back pocket and placed it on the ground.

"So, have we had a quiet soul-lifting day?" She asked.

"Perfect. It seems so remote I can just imagine Nuja grazing across the land."

"Uh uh." She straightened up from her task. "You said no horses. No mention of horses."

She walked over and sat down beside him, snuggling under his arm as he made room. There they sat while the silence, or perhaps the fogs of time, almost audible, seeped in.

"It does seem timeless, doesn't it?" She asked. "Nuja and his pale mare might have grazed here, freed for the night when their packs were removed. We walked in two miles from the highway. We could be on ground they walked across."

Bridger felt a momentary excitement. "They weren't in the Caledonia brigade, though," he admitted. "Theirs was the Snake expedition – as much as a hundred and seventy years ago. This is no more than a hundred and forty, about."

"But then they came?"

"Oh, yes."

"A hundred and forty, hundred and seventy – but a day, a minute in the life of a mountain," Louise thought. She looked at the mountain looming ahead, the others folding behind, as though enclosing this little spot protectively while the night went by and morning came. Do they still hold the vibrations? It seems, if we are very quiet, we can hear the munching of grass, soft snorts, faint voices.

Suddenly she roused herself from the pervading mood. "Let's get back to our time," she said, "before I slip completely into your remote world. Maybe that's why you're so distant."

"Distant? I'm not distant!"

"Yes, you are. You hang off from the heart of things."

"We've been just the two of us all day, heart to heart. That's not distant," he protested.

"Yes, but I have to pursue you, entice you, court you!"

Bridger's face waxed solemn. "Listen, I have to tell you something."

"I know."

"You know?"

"I know what you're going to say. Kitty told me about the M.S. She didn't tell me deliberately," she hastened to explain. "It was a slip. It doesn't matter to me what you've got, Bridge. Don't shut me out because of that," she pleaded as his face mirrored a series of emotions. "Lots of people have serious ailments to deal with."

"As if I didn't know," he retorted. "Mackie…"

"What happened to Mackie?"

"He died."

"Of M.S.?" she asked, startled.

"No. Of cancer."

"I'm sorry. You were childhood friends?"

"No. I met him after I arrived in Toronto. We were compatible opposites. We were about twenty and had the tipsy world by the tail. It just seemed we did everything together, the good and the bad. We got our first jobs there together. He got married. I got married. Then, as the world sobered, he got divorced. I got divorced. He got cancer. I got M.S. We were always there for each other. And then he died – and I didn't."

"Is that why you wouldn't go for further treatment? You didn't try to get any better."

"Of course I tried to get better! Believe me, no one sits and just accepts the pain and the disability. I was getting better, slowly."

"But psychologically, you felt guilty because you were alive?"

"No. I felt it was unfair. Now I feel guilty."

"Now! Why?"

"Because you're here, like sunshine all about me." Louise's face lit up and immediately fell as he went on. "But I couldn't let you walk into a situation like this. I don't know what will happen in the future."

"I didn't walk in, Bridger. At any rate, no matter what you fear might happen, I won't walk out. I couldn't."

He looked squarely at her for a few seconds, then, suddenly relinquishing his logical stand, said, "No, I know. We couldn't walk away from each other."

He picked up his wallet and she watched him study the little fancywork picture, so incomprehensibly important to him (and somehow to her). What was the irresistible link that this represented?

"And I'm grateful for that," he went on, "because I couldn't bear the thought of not having you in my life."

The words she wanted to hear! They strummed in her head like musical chords.

"There he is, Louise! He's come back!" Rillas shouted. Louise came out of the barn with pieces of tack in her hands.

"He's there, he's there!" her father was yelling and waving excitedly.

Louise walked quickly along the front of the barn, turned and went along the end to the fence rail. From there, the view was straight across the field and up the mountainside.

"Where?" she asked.

"There!" he fumed. "Wait till he comes out more from the trees." He handed her the magnifying glasses he had in his hand "I'll get that bastard. Look at him! He just stands there, defiantly."

"Gee, Dad," said Louise, studying the horse closely, "he isn't a nag at all. He's got good conformation."

Rillas cast her a look of utter frustration. "Don't you ever stick to the point?" He spluttered, and gyrated off, seemingly trying to go in two directions at once.

Louise put the glasses to her face again and studied the beast. He didn't make the slightest move, just stood gazing steadily down, and she felt locked in his gaze.

She lowered the glasses at a muffled sound. Snow was coming across the field at a slow trot, her head lifting enquiringly. The grey had made no sound, but something bespoke his presence. He moved into cover but she had caught a glimpse.

She raced around in a circle, then raised herself slightly on her hind legs to bring the front ones down again. Her eyes bored into the spot on the hill. She was unsure now, but making light whinnies and moving restively, lifting one foot and then the other while she searched the hill.

"Oh, Snow." The words escaped softly from Louise's lips.

For the next two days, Rillas stayed glued to Richard, keeping him practising, perfecting. He continued expostulating as Richard, deciding finality, walked Snow to the gate and dismounted.

"No more!" He said forcefully, opened the gate, led her through and down to the barn, took off the saddle and bridle, all the while trading irritabilities with his father. Louise put the halter on Snow and started brushing her down. The other two left, bickering.

Everyone was tense! Snow stood, for the moment, passive, but at other times restive. When she was outside, her eyes constantly searched the hillside. For Louise, the tension twisted inside her continually as she thought of her illogical actions – the preparations she had made to get Snow away safely. To her father, this would be absurdity; more, treachery! Yet, all she knew was that Snow would go, regardless, bidden by the call of centuries.

CHAPTER SEVEN

There was a good crowd in the stands and around the fences for this medium-sized derby. The riders in their sleek pants, well-cut jackets, high riding boots, velvet helmets, looked quite impressive.

Bridger hadn't really wanted to come.

"Of course you have to go," Kitty had insisted. "Louise wants you to be there."

"If her father sees any of us, it will make things worse for her and for him, too," he had protested.

"Well, you two stay out of his way. I'll get to see Louise."

The horses were beautiful. Each one doing its solo performance was worthy of a trophy, Bridger thought. Richard had the two horses again in the competition: the black horse, glossy black except for an exploding star on her forehead, and Snow. Richard felt mixed emotions about riding Snow. Her small size diminished his ego, but her independent spirit challenged his skill in handling, and she was certainly challenging it today!

"Queen of the Niger," the announcer intoned. "A clean ride."

"Nice ride," Kitty said.

"Very nice," Arnie seconded. "*One* of his horses, is co-operating."

During the show, Bridger caught sight of Chick in the crowd. He recognised Malcolm and his son, and on asking Arnie about the fourth member, "That's Malcolm's father," he replied. "He raises horses with Malcolm. Or rather, Malcolm raises horses with him, although Malcolm has other horses of his own. Braid imports horses from Ireland and England. Rillas has bought horses from him."

"Oh!" Bridger expressed some surprise.

"That horse of Chick's came from the Braid stables."

"Chase?"

"Yeah."

"How came Rillas didn't buy him? He's a beauty."

"He's not a jumper – not that kind of jumper. He's a working hunter. Sort of an Irish specialty."

"Kind of an expensive horse for Chick, isn't he?"

"Yes, but it had some defect to do with its legs. They usually put them down, but Braid thought it would outgrow it, and it did. Still it had to be gelded and couldn't be registered. He made him train with the horse, and he made him do a little dressage – to Chick's displeasure – as well as the general equestrian, because the horse was a natural for it. That was years ago. Chick won junior trophies. I don't know what he's done since."

"But he's doing this demonstration tomorrow, at this 'every horse' thing."

"All horse," Arnie corrected. "Yes. I meant competitively. He's been going along in the practices, in the training of Malcolm's son, Gabriel, and Malcolm's mother asked him to do this demonstration with Gabriel just to give him company and confidence. But they really want Chick to get in there, too. "Malcolm says Chick is pleased that he was asked, but he'd never admit it. He's been sullen and cynical since he lost his job two or three years ago."

"What was his job?" Bridger asked.

"Surveying, but he got restructured out of it."

"Well, I guess you can understand his lack of spontaneity."

"Yes, but his aunt says they need to develop some diplomatic ways in him."

"Diplomatic ways! High-sounding words for developing a little amenability," Bridger said. "Besides, he isn't that bad."

"That's because the two of you – who can figure out why – strike a sympathetic chord."

"Yes, but they seem to be constantly circling him. He's, ironically, more like the besieged wagon train. Are they protecting him or impounding him? Do you think they secretly tend to embrace this White Wolf thing?" Bridger asked archly. "What are the subtle signs that attach to him?"

As Arnie guffawed, Bridger went on, "What's it like to be a chief in this time?"

"Well," Arnie returned, "you know he can't be a hereditary chief, so if he's destined for chieftainship of any kind, it's in the stars."

"Yes," Bridger said with a rise in voice, "indicated by a grey horse maybe?"

"You talk nuts," Arnie rejoined.

All the while, people were walking horses back and forth behind them as they stood at the fence. One horse nibbled grass while his owner talked with an acquaintance drinking coffee from a plastic cup. Far off, in another area, contestants were circling in a different competition. Bridger moved his attention from scene to scene, while the next jumper entered and got his signal. Except for his worry over Snow's recalcitrant behaviour, he was beginning to feel bored, and it wasn't even halfway through yet! When a break did come, Arnie raced off for coffee. Bridger stayed put, fearing they'd never find each other for the rest of the afternoon.

When the trials started again, however, they were all back in their places.

"I had a coffee with Louise," Kitty said. A minute later she gave Bridger a poke. "There," she said, and pointed. "Louise is waving."

Away off, she stood waving with both arms. Bridger waved back and clasped his hands together in a triumphal gesture.

"I hope she got that moral support," he said, as Snow started.

"She did," Kitty assured him, "and she needs it. She knows your signal was for safe results, not for the trophy. She's worried Snow will hurt herself and Richard... and look at Snow! She's taking those jumps with a fury. It's all Richard can do to hold her. What will she do at this water gate coming up?"

"She's refused it," Arnie said. "He has to take her back."

"She *could* do it," Kitty said. "No, she won't. And look at her. She's racing off beyond! She's disqualified."

"Look, she's turning back," Arnie said. "Surely she's not going to take that jump from the other side!"

"Oh, God! Louise!" Kitty exclaimed in the same terror she knew the other must be feeling.

"He's there," Bridger said.

"Who's there?" Arnie asked.

"The grey. He's running beside her, parallel to her on clear ground."

"Are you crazy? There's no horse there. She'll hit that fence!"

"No," Bridger said with sudden calm, "she's got directed power, now."

Snow's forefeet touched the edge of the water, her hind legs pushed powerfully and she rose like a kite in an updraft, then took the ground on the other side of the gate with strong recovery and deftly veered off the course.

"She must be built like a spaceship," Arnie said, breathing again, along with Kitty. "She can spin on a shoenail and go straight up and down."

"Nuja took her over," Bridger said very soberly.

Arnie, whatever his thoughts, had no retort to make.

Later, as the crowd began to leave, Bridger steered for Chick's party. Much of the talk in the crowd was still of the incredible defeat.

The older Braid was still shaking his head. "A most perverse lady," he said.

"And she recovered herself," Malcolm added.

"And the rider stayed on!" Chick added further. Deserved praise for Richard.

As the parties moved off, Kitty looked back to see Chick and Bridger lagging behind. After a short conversation Chick hurried after his party, and in a few steps Bridger overtook her. They exchanged a knowing look (despite herself, Kitty was now seriously converted to Bridger's belief) and went on to find Arnie, who was in conversation with someone ahead.

When they arrived home, Bridger changed clothes and did a few tasks. He grabbed a piece of ham as Kitty was slicing it for supper, and went out the door, waving her car keys at her. She acknowledged with a worried nod.

All the way up the valley, the sun was a red ball in the rear view mirror, but it slipped below the horizon before he reached his destination. Chick's truck was already there. Bridger made his way down.

"It's all quiet," Chick said as Bridger reached him. "They had Snow in that field with the black horse for a while, then Louise came out and put her in the barn. Her dad was so excited when they came in, I could hear him from here. He was all hyped up and ready to put her in the next International show even though she'd been disqualified on every rule in the book."

Bridger laughed. "Louise said he'd be acting that way." Then in a change of tone he said, "And I thought *you* said the grey wouldn't let Snow see him till this event was over."

"I thought he wouldn't," Chick answered.

"He put her into a complete frenzy," Bridger accused, and Chick nodded guiltily.

"But look how beautifully he pulled her out of it," he defended. "You saw him, too, didn't you?"

"Yes," Bridger admitted. "I saw him, too."

Chick nodded, then turned to their mission. "You're right about the fences," he said. "There's a barbed wire fence behind the blackberry and other growth, and someone's cut most of the growth away behind, just leaving the front cover towards the house. Did Louise do that?"

"Her mother had the gardener do it, while Louise made sure her father had business away from the house. She has an ally in her mother, and the gardener wouldn't tell – she said she heard him chuckling to himself. So now we've got to finish cutting the blackberry vines through, cut the wires away, and get that post out. And it's got to go. Or else the tree. I don't think we can take on the tree. She's left lots of tools. Damn! We can't work till it's nearly dark. How are we going to see?"

"The moon is already high," Chick said, "and it's clear. We'll see enough. We can probably cut the wire now and get it out of the way. There's enough cover if we stay low."

After they'd done that, there was nothing to do but sit and wait.

"Funny this, isn't it?" Chick said. "Here we are working together to pay off a debt incurred centuries ago." After a moment he said, "You know, when I first used to see you I never expected to get to know you. You were so withdrawn."

"*I* was!" Bridger exclaimed, accounting that was the second time he'd been told. "I thought that of you."

Chick looked over with a touch of amusement. "That's the gentlest term that's ever been applied to me."

"Would you like to be a chief?" Bridger asked abruptly.

"Oh, you're thinking of that White Wolf thing that certain ones deny and wistfully hope for," Chick, still amused, answered with quick grasp. "To be a chief two hundred years ago, in white deer-skins, on a horse with streamers flying and the braves coursing beside – yes. Yes! Wouldn't you?" He prodded a smile onto Bridger's face. "As for White Wolf, he probably would have liked that, too, but our bands hadn't got horses at that time. They had dugouts and canoes, and farther down, vines to climb the walls of the canyons."

"A resourceful mode of passage," Bridger interjected. "What skill and courage!"

"Yeah," Chick broke off, "I wouldn't like to do it today. And I would never be, or wish to be, material for any White Wolf today."

After a moment he said, "Do you ever think of Sackasack?"

Bridger got the association immediately – forbidding Sackasack.

"Sometimes," Chick went on, "I could feel the driving intent of him, and the anger. Who was he avenging? Was it worth it when the few remaining limped home with him?"

"Maybe time moulded him into a good chief, maybe a great chief," Bridger philosophised.

"Or maybe he didn't get home," Chick said. "Did you? Did I? I keep thinking I didn't. Did you take that long trail back without me?"

"I don't know," Bridger said, shaking his head. "I don't know."

Soon the darkness folded in, but the moon, bright on the field, allowed them to see through the remaining vines.

Even with jackets and gloves, the thorns attacked the exposed parts of their arms, and their faces.

"What a rotten job this is," Chick said.

"This may be the easy part," Bridger answered. "Wait till we get to the post."

They cut through the last vines, and the moon lit a path straight through.

"Okay, the post!" They took up the shovels and began to dig. The ground wouldn't give. "Try the picks!"

Rocks and pebbles gave most reluctantly and slowly around the post. "Let's try the mallets." They took turns giving it blows. "Boy, it's as solid as cement."

"No, it's giving, it's giving."

"But not easily. Try the pick again. It's loosening more."

"Here's the grey." Chick made out the dark shape. "He's coming to this spot. I hope he'll stay patiently."

"Make him," Bridger said with urgency. "You understand him."

"No. Oh, no. I retract that rash presumption that I could know Tnustchaen." He moved a few feet back as the grey came up calmly and even allowed a tentative hand on his mane. Bridger began making more headway with the post. Then a whinny sounded in the clear air.

"Oh, God! Snow knows he's here," Chick said. "Someone's running across the concourse to the barn. It's Louise."

The whinnying from the barn grew more frantic. The grey gave an answering call. Chick's grasp on the mane tightened, and he was almost lifted off his feet. Exerting all his strength and speaking Indian words, he stayed him, while Bridger, taking the mallet, pounded feverishly at the post.

"She's out!" Chick said. "She's coming straight towards us." Bridger could now hear the pounding hooves above his own laboured breathing. Concerting all his energies, he aimed one mighty blow at the resistant post. The grey bolted past the tree, past Bridger, and swerved up the trail. The post gave, and Bridger went with it. As his body hit the ground, Snow was over clear, and racing up the trail behind the grey.

"God, that was close," Bridger said as he rolled over and sat up, spitting out dirt. "I thought my arms would fly off and go with the mallet in those last seconds."

As the sounds of the pounding hooves and their passage through the scrub faded away, Bridger thought he should be feeling at least a sense of satisfaction, but instead the silence seemed desolate.

"Where will they go?" He asked.

"I don't know. To the hills! To far meadows! That's where I'd go," Chick answered.

After a moment he said, "You know, we always thought Tnustchaen wanted to go back to where we knew he had come from, but if he's the horse of endless centuries, I think it doesn't matter where he was, it's where he is – he's following her, his Snow, his Princessa, his one love."

Bridger nodded in the dark. "If they make it free, will she survive? No barns, no vets, no hay," he persisted.

"Well, she's healthy. If the weather doesn't get harsh too quickly, she'll become seasoned to it. They'll be alright!" He added with confidence, in an effort to assuage Bridger's unease. "Look! We were required to provide her safe escape. We're not asked to protect their wild existence, or even worry about it. We performed the task assigned to us. It wasn't voluntary."

"Of course you're right!" Bridger acknowledged.

"How are we going to put this fence back together?" Chick turned to the task to be done.

"We can't. Louise said to leave it. They wouldn't put any horses in here till they fix the fence."

"Thank goodness for that!" Chick said. "How'd you get Louise to go along with this, anyway?"

"I didn't. She made her own plans after she saw the grey one day. She didn't know why, but she knew she had to let Snow go. Brainwashed, you might say, in one two-minute session."

Chick nodded with understanding. "Her assignment."

"Yes," Bridger acknowledged, thinking of Rosalita's words: "Whoever owes him will help him despite themselves."

Pushing himself up, he groaned with the effort. "Boy, my arms are just weak with that final pounding. Same with you?" He asked as Chick rubbed at his arms.

"Yeah. My muscles feel like a thousand electric impulses are shooting through them, especially in my right arm."

"I hope that disappears by tomorrow;" Bridger said.

"So do I. So do I."

CHAPTER EIGHT

Having bowed to the appropriate districts for the dressage, and almost unrecognisable in the bowler hat 'Chick kept any tension he might have felt, under a calm control'. Bridger noticed, though, that he pressed, at his arm rather often.

"It'll be alright," he said as Bridger questioned him. Bridger went to the stands and joined Arnie and Kitty for Chick's and Gabriel's ride.

Horses and riders moved smoothly forward, each at his own end. Down the centre of their respective squares, turn right, to the corner, right again and up to the top, turn right and diagonal trot, turn again.

"They just keep going around," Bridger said.

"It's more than that," Kitty said.

"Yeah, soon they'll do their pirouette," Arnie said, making circling motions with his fingers.

"Oh!" Kitty pushed at him. "They're not into that. Cut it out, Arnie." She turned to Bridger. "When they're being judged – and they're not – they have to be seen from every angle. The horses' bodies must be perfectly aligned in the direction of the movement to maintain perfect balance and smoothness. And all done without apparent effort, and with only the barest control of the reins.

"I do see that," Bridger said. "He sure regained perfection in these few weeks."

"Oh, he probably practises at home," Kitty said.

"Does he?"

"He must, to be that good."

"Sooo," Bridger drew the word out, "that takes a lot of patience and dedication?"

"Sure thing. See how much more smoothly Chick's horse moves. 'Collected' is the term."

Just a moment after that, Chick's arm jerked so hard it reined Chase's head sharply and pulled him out of step. The crowd gasped, and Gabriel faltered.

"What!" Kitty exclaimed.

"Christ Almighty!" Arnie exclaimed.

Even Bridger knew that action didn't belong in the performance, but they horses continued even though Gabriel cast an inquiring glance.

"Oh, damn," Arnie said. "He did it again. Not nearly so bad, though, but Chick looks as though he might bolt out of there."

Bridger held his breath, fearing just that as Arnie talked on. "He's putting both reins in his left hand. He's not supposed to do that. He's letting Chase take it." His voice lightened as he said, "Let's see if we were right about, Chase."

Bridger exhaled as Chick said something to Gabriel and the two continued. With only the leg-pressures, Chase took up the pattern effortlessly. On into circles, into figures-of-eight.

"See them change lead?" Kitty pointed out.

"No," Bridger answered. "When do they do that?"

"In the cross of the eight. See. Oh!" Kitty gave up. "Now they're coming around again and approaching each other to turn and salute. Gabriel gave a creditable performance, and Chase showed the absolute fluidity of his natural movement."

The two doffed their hats, then turned and trotted out to the crowd's sincere applause.

Bridger left to go down to Chick and Gus slipped into his seat. "What happened to Chick in there?" He asked. "I was sitting next to the man who judged the other classes. He was remarking on everything – correct flexion, smooth transition, beautiful movement – then Chick went nuts!"

"Yeah," Arnie said. "I don't understand what happened, but anyway it looks like Chase retrieved his honour."

However that may have been, the disappointment and self-assumed humiliation still showed in Chick's face and he refused to be consoled by all who observed to him that it wasn't all that bad. "We know why it happened," they said. "The rest was good."

"Well, sometimes it goes that way," Malcolm finally said, rather brutally. "It was only a horse ride after all, Chick."

Later in the day Chick's better nature returned and he even entered a couple of unofficial events. Bridger was glad to see his lightening of mood and said so. "You looked so angry in those moments I was afraid you'd go, off and..."

"And what?" Chick asked as Bridger searched for words. "Scalp someone?"

Bridger burst into laughter at that. "I was afraid," he said, moderating his voice, "You'd stomp off and glower on the side-lines. I was glad you stayed with it. The crowd admired you even if they didn't understand, and they loved your horse."

"Oh, spare me! You sound just like my relatives. Look, they're waving me back now. Guess I'd better go over there and do something civilised before them – like smiling."

Bridger was the one who smiled as Chick walked off, straight-faced.

The next morning Louise drove in.

"Did you forget the kids are back in school?" Bridger asked.

"No, I didn't forget. I came to take you home with me. Oh, Dad's not home," she added, as he immediately resisted. "He'll probably be away all day. He was gone all day yesterday, looking for Snow. I looked for Snow yesterday, myself."

At Bridger's startled look she explained. "No, I'm not trying to get her back. I'd just like to know where she is, that she's okay. Yesterday, I thought, she could be just up above the road, in the bush up there. I spent two hours hiking through there. Then I went and got the car, and looked at all the farms within a few miles."

"Do you think they'd stay close around?" Bridger asked.

"No. I don't know."

"What would you do if you found her? What would you do if your father found her?"

She drew in her breath. "I don't want him to find her. I want her free. But I want to know she's okay."

"Okay, I'll tell Kitty," Bridger said sympathetically. If he could feel that dispiriting dissatisfaction he had the other night, how much more deeply must she feel it?

On the way up, she made a few little side excursions into dead-end roads.

"Do you really think they'd be down this way?" He asked. "Chick says the grey would head for wilderness –

and that they'll be okay. I think Snow will be okay," he added, taking on Chick's reassuring tone.

Drifting on the thought, Bridger believed what Chick had said. Nuja had once again collected his pale mare. He had protected her and lost her on the North West Cordillera before, but he had found her right here on the Cordillera again. Maybe even – maybe Nuja *was* that horse that fled limping into the mountains of New Mexico with the yellow mare at his heels; that screamed his despair on the wharf at Seville as the waters separated him from his Princessa; that streaked across the sands of Africa to find his mate in another camp.

"That horse wouldn't linger close to the domains of men," Bridger thought, "once it became unnecessary."

He glanced at Louise, who remained riveted to the steering wheel as the miles passed. "I wonder what we owed him for?" He asked himself, "she and I?"

CHAPTER NINE

Arnie had the rest of September to go to his horse and pony clubs. There were two fairs and one last meet; the same applied for Malcolm. Chick was staying for these and for the Indian rodeo at the end of the month. For all of them, it still meant combing and washing, loading and driving, saddling and tethering, baking in the hot sun through a slow parade, plumping for Maggie doing a key-hole in drizzling rain, while her pony tried to head for shelter.

The Indian rodeo was like all rodeos – noisy and dusty. Ribbons and trophies attested to the rough and tough skills of the contestants, who all – riders and horses – became more dusted and sweated as the day wore on, though they had started out polished and neat.

When the event ended, Bridger went seeking Chick to say goodbye. He also had some tantalising information. As he searched through the crowd, he heard his name called. He turned to see Chick making his way towards him. "I've been looking for you," he said.

They engaged in small talk about the performances and ribbons and trophies. Finally, Chick held out his hand and Bridger took it.

"Well," said Chick, "goodbye Lachwalkie."

The name flowed slowly into Bridger's consciousness – yes, that's what he was called. He struggled to remember the name that was Chick's, but couldn't. Feelingly he said, "Goodbye, Chick," but it came out, "Otono."

Otono!

Chick grinned. "I won't forget you."

"Friends for hundreds of years." Bridger returned. "How could we forget each other?"

"One more thing," Bridger said as they dropped hands. "I think you'll be interested in this. We may have a sighting on the horses. Marda, a friend of Kitty's, told her the other day, that a relative of hers has been driving a logging truck far out of Chilliwack. One day last week, he saw far off on a rocky ridge, two whitish animals. He got rather excited because he thought they might be mountain sheep or goats (which don't inhabit the area). He caught sight of them a couple more times as the road wound, then lost sight of them altogether, until many, many miles on when he rounded a bend and saw the animals again. They were quite some distance away but he could see them clearly on the flat of a lower mountain: they were horses, and they must have been close to the rocky edge at his first sighting.

"He didn't think it was part of a ranch – although miles back there had been a ranch. It was all up and down. There were no other horses or cattle anywhere. It seemed complete wilderness. What especially struck Marda was that he said one of them, the whiter one, was rather elegant looking, like a show horse. Marda told Kitty because she and Kitty have been putting together the grey horse's exploits. Marda's the one who rooted out the brigade accounts for us."

"So," Bridger said with a flourish, "do I detect a tinge of interest?"

"Intense interest," Chick, said. "I'd like to see that son-of-a-gun. But what are you thinking?"

"Louise and Kitty want to go and see if it's them. Louise has to see."

Chick nodded to that. "Just to see?"

"Yes."

"I'd like to see, too. Very much. But how close could we get and will they still be there?"

"Well, you'd have to see them and make a plan."

Chick nodded and then said, "I haven't heard anything about them since that day. How'd her father take the affair?"

"Very angrily, and he vows to catch Nuja and get Snow back. Of course Louise isn't telling him about this sighting."

"No worry," Chick laughed. "*Nobody* catches the grey horse."

With Arnie shaking his head from the doorway (bunch of nuts! Let a good horse run into the wilds and then go looking for it), Kitty and Bridger left with one horse in the truck. They would meet Chick, with Chase and one of Malcolm's horses in his truck, then go to pick up Louise and her horse.

Bridger had balked when they mentioned horses. (Haw! She thinks she'll make him a rider after they're married, Arnie chuckled to himself.) "I thought we could see them from the road."

"Yes, but if we can't, we've got to go in with horses."

"We could just hike in."

"If it's not too far."

"We can't go in too far, anyway," Bridger admonished. "Do you know the country?"

Chick admitted he didn't.

"Louise has been in," Kitty said.

"Only once, with her dad and some other ranchers," Bridger reminded them.

"But I remember it well," Louise said. "Besides, we have to venture a little." The other two agreed.

"Well, if you have to use horses, I'll stay at the road," Bridger said. A chorus of "No" answered that.

"You can ride," Louise declared.

"I'll give you Pinjam," Kitty said. "And Malcolm will let you bring Tasha?" She turned to Chick, who nodded.

"I used to ride Tasha a lot when Harfelts had her. Malcolm bought Tasha from Harfelts," she explained.

"Okay, then," Louise took it up, "I'll take Ditmar, my faithful little gelding, and he'll be alright with Pinjam."

It was a long ride and the second half of the road was gravel, which got rougher and rougher. Finally they got to the spot where they could park their vehicles off the road. Marda's relative had drawn a map for them. The spot from where he had seen the horses was about a half-mile farther along. They got out and walked up the road. There was no mistaking the spot marked X. The view swept away in a panorama of hills beyond hills. The first days of October, and the sun still soaked the land in summer heat. The trees were like great flowering bushes, golden and orange leaved. Snatches of red bush flamed low along the ground. Yet the high peaks had a dusting of snow.

"They must have been right there on the first hill," Chick said. "He said he could discern them clearly. And there's the ridge of rock, on the far edge. They couldn't have gone too far."

"Do you recognise anything?" Kitty asked Louise.

"Yes, I think I do. We head straight over those hills from where we left the trucks. They're just about there above that wedge of trees."

They went back and saddled the horses, all the while Bridger hiding his nervousness. Chick went to check the first part. He came back to say that, as Louise had said, they had to go down a small ravine and up the other side, then the ground lay open.

The three riders walked their horses carefully down the ravine. It was an easy slope, nothing like the steep grade above the Rillas estate. Bridger took his horse by the reins and walked down, constantly looking back and keeping a little to the side, lest (so he feared) the horse walk over him. Out of the trees, the ground rose. Not until he reached the crest would Bridger get on.

But what a view greeted them. The land stretched flat and grassy ahead, the sun lying upon it like a golden sheet. Of one impulse, the three riders spurred their horses and raced ahead, leaving Bridger to hold back Pinjam (who wanted to run with the troop) to a reluctant walk. At the far side, the riders halted and waited a little guiltily while Bridger made slow passage. Before he got there, he had been forced to allow PinJam a slow trot, which jiggled him like Arnie's old mower. It didn't please Pinjam much, either.

As they assembled again, Louise said, "I think I remember. We go down this grade, up that rise, and around the side of that hill."

The others went easily down the slope, while Bridger reined close to keep Pinjam from breaking into a run, then through open trees at the bottom. Up the other side was just as bad. Pinjam had to have some speed, but not too much or she'd bounce him right out of the saddle. "Oh, God. Why did I agree to this?" Bridger agonised. Around the side of the mountain turned out to be a gradual ascent, for they came easily onto another crest. In little dips, it rolled gently far ahead. This time they all kept their horses to a walk.

"If it would only stay like this," Bridger thought. The hooves clopped softly. Stray breezes bent the grasses as they moved under the lazy sun. Louise was ahead of him; she had on faded blue jeans and a paste checked shirt. Bridger watched the supple movements of her body as the horse moved. He seemed to see a girl in buckskins, bare brown legs against a mottled fawn hide. Black hair hung over her ears in two pigtails tied with strips of something – probably deerhide or rabbit skin. The dark head turned to look back at him, but the face was indistinct. The scene ended abruptly, and Louise was looking back at him.

"Yeah," he said with immediate presence, "I'm still here."

She smiled and turned her back, but slowed to proceed silently beside him.

"'Funny," she thought. "This is somehow familiar."

It wasn't like any trail ride she had ever been on – far more distant than that. Horses moving easily, unhurried. It was as though she had crossed a land like this before. Slow-paced but purposeful. She could almost hear voices, children's voices among them. The sense was so strong it was like a murmur in her head...

Chick and Kitty had cantered ahead. Louise focused to see them tracking toward the bluff. When they disappeared she cast a hopeful look at Bridger.

"Go!" He said. Without hesitation she took off at a gallop after them. When she gained sight of them, Kitty was looking over to another hill. Chick had searched out the farther frontier and was coming back. "Too rough that way," he said.

"Which way then?"

"Let's wait till Bridger gets up," Louise said, and when he did, "The straightforward way looks over that hill, but I don't think I've been there."

"Oh, no!" Groaned Bridger. "That's a long way down and a long way up the other side, and then what?"

"Yes, let's not go too far," Kitty said. "I don't want to get lost in these mountains."

They stood in indecision. All wanted to see what they had come for, but Bridger was unwilling to go any farther on a horse. Chick was eager to go a little farther. Louise ardently wished for a sight of her horse. Bridger knew she would opt to go on, but Kitty's sense of caution over-ruled her keen desire to see the horses. She looked at the time of day: the sun was already in its diurnal descent. Any little incident could keep them in these hills after darkness fell.

"It wouldn't take long to get over there," Louise said wistfully.

"No, but by the time Bridger got over there, it would," Kitty said, "We've been over two hours going in. Remember, we have to go back, too!"

Bridger took the criticism stoically, but looking at Louise's crestfallen face, said, "I could stay here and the rest of you could ride over. I'll sit and eat the sandwiches while you're gone."

Ignoring his humour, they pondered this suggestion.

"I don't know," Kitty said. She, too, felt for Louise's disappointment, but then she said decisively, "I say, no."

As they eyed each other, she said, "Remember we promised to stay together on this. No one goes alone and the party doesn't split up."

"Besides," Chick said, taking on some of Kitty's caution, "That wooded area could hide some difficult terrain. I don't think we have the time to explore. We don't even know if that's the right direction to explore. We've gone generally east. They could be south in Whatcom county by now."

Reluctantly the riders yielded to their own rule. Bridger breathed a sigh of relief. He knew where he was in relation to the road. He knew it visually. He spoke this aloud. "We only have to go back around this bluff and we can see where we've come from, straight across two hills."

"But there's a lot of twisting and turning and up and down," Kitty said.

"And I also made a little map, using bold landmarks," he continued.

"Good," she said. "We'll see how it checks out with the compass map I've been keeping.

"Yes. We'll see if it works," Louise said. "I've never used a compass before."

"Arnie made me bring it," Kitty said. "But it's an extra. I'm trusting to my visual and memory senses. How about you Chick?"

"Oh, natural instinct, of course," he gave a little laugh.

When they got to the round of the bluff and could see the lay of their passage back, Louise first, then the others, turned their horses toward the wilderness and sat looking at the beckoning hills, the empty beckoning hills.

Bridger, eager to be on the way, finally made a suggestion of departure. Kitty and Louise acceded and started to turn their horses.

Chick said, "Look!" His eyes were riveted on a wooded spot up the far hill to the right. "There!" He pointed, trying to make the others see. They strained, but could see nothing, even with the glasses which Kitty brought out of her saddlebag. After a few minutes they made motions of leaving.

"No," said Bridger, now unwilling to leave. "If Chick sees something, there's something there."

"They're grazing," Chick said. "They're moving out slowly."

The three novices at forest sight strained hopelessly.

"Are you sure you're not seeing a stump?" Louise asked. "I can't see a darn thing. Oh! I can. It moved." She went into a gyration of arm moving, trying to make the others see, then called excitedly, "Snow! Snow!"

The sound reverberated from hill to hill: Snow! Snow! Snow! Snow! repeated fainter and fainter.

The outburst startled the others and even the horses. Some of them moved, and Bridger grabbed to make the reins short, but unflappable Pinjam didn't move.

"Patience!" Chick admonished. "They're moving down."

"Now you learn the Indian art of stoic endurance," Bridger said. Although he spoke lightly, he remembered soberly the long waits in covert positions, and the body-aching immovability.

Presently, a very definite form moved out of the tree cover. "I see it," Kitty said, looking through the glasses.

"It's the grey! Oh, they've got to come closer than that! Snow has to come out of there!"

"She will eventually," Chick said. "I think she heard her, name three or four dozen times."

Ages and ages it seemed, while Kitty and Louise passed the glasses back and forth, before the horses came fully into the open. Then they meandered down the long gradual slope, pausing now and again, and raising their heads high in that sniffing gesture, to look in the watchers' direction, until finally they stood in bold relief across the chasm of the hill: two horses, their coats well dusted with dried mud, manes caught up tightly in burrs.

"That's Snow?" Louise gasped.

They all gazed silently for a few moments.

"Boy, their winter coats are coming in good," Kitty said.

"How can you tell?" Bridger asked.

"Look at the outer frame against the light. See the long hairs."

"Oh, yeah," Bridger said in a rise of tone.

Suddenly, as though she had made her goodbyes, Snow broke into a run. The grey followed. From the far right, the horses galloped across to the far left, and then down a little bit of a hill. At the bottom they stopped and rolled in a patch of bare ground to collect some fresh dirt. They could see the white underbelly of one. Then back up the little hill and onto the long brow, turning, and down again, and up.

"She's where she wants to be," Louise admitted to herself and felt the first real sense of peace about her she had for a month.

Snow had come only halfway up the little hill before circling back, but the grey had come right up onto the brow and stood facing the four across the space of hills. He seemed to be looking straight at Chick.

"Are you thinking you owe him," Bridger asked silently, "for some of those hard knocks?"

Suddenly a pure white horse stood on the slope beyond. With prancing feet she came forward. Her rider wore white deerskins. White fur tails and feathers adorned his headdress. He brought the horse forward and turned to a halt. The horse stood a little restlessly while the rider scanned some unseen horizon.

"That's Snow," Louise exclaimed.

"That's Chick," Kitty exclaimed. "Older and impressive, Wow!"

Bridger shot a glance to his left. There stood Chase, rider-less, but only briefly. Chick was back in the saddle even as Kitty was exclaiming again.

"Look at that headdress," she said. "It's changing. It's becoming shiny, silvery, like a very fine helmet – with furs and feathers attached so they cascade down one side. And the tunic, though fringed, is cut close; the pants are tailored and fit into those boots."

"And have you ever seen boots like that before?" Bridger broke in. "The moccasins have streamlined into very supple-looking, very fine boots. And look at the red blanket – no saddle." And that's not Chick anymore," Kitty stressed. "What's that insignia on the breast of the tunic? Can't make it out because he's turned. Looks like a petroglyph in red. Red braid."

"Symbols of some power. Red and white," Bridger murmured, thinking of Malcolm's legend. And behind there seemed the sounds of bands and the ghost of flags of nations. Rather un-Indian-like.

"Great Sachem," Kitty murmured back.

"This may be the new White Wolf, not yet known, perhaps not yet born," Bridger's voice fell even softer.

Louise finally broke into their duet. "What is this?" she asked incredulously.

"I think it's a legend that will take place sometime," Bridger said. "Sometime."

Like a bubble breaking, the beautiful picture was gone. Chick sat his horse as though he had never moved, but he knew what had just happened. More sober than in his soberest moments, he remained a few seconds locked in the grey's steady gaze.

What prodigious lessons had Nuja taught him in those quick tastes of glory? And what was his connection to this foretold leader of a great domain?

As quickly and as disinterestedly, the grey unlocked his gaze. Then he turned and raced down the hill past Snow and up to the top of the other side, where he waited for her to join him. Like two yearlings, they raced off, taking wide circles away from each other, then narrowing in and running close. The pass ahead of them rose in a little ascent, then rounded away out of the vision of the watchers. Without slowing a whit, they raced up and curved out of sight.

A chieftain and his queen.

ABOUT THE AUTHOR

What can I say? To dabble at writing for nigh on fifty years and then to write a story and have it accepted and published. Inexpressible!

What did I do through all of those years? There was the usual home and family with all that pertains to that, such as, in my case, lots and lots of sewing. Then there was the side interest of night school and correspondence courses. Also there were spurts and lags of good health and poor health. Still, I kept scribbling to have, at this date, something, however anyone views it, to show for it.